THRILL IN THE 'VILLE

By Patsi B. Trollinger
Illustrated by Elizabeth Thompson

Patsi B. Trollinger

BENJAMIN PRESS

This book is dedicated to every young reader and future voter.
- P.B.T.

BENJAMIN PRESS

135 North Second Street
Danville, Kentucky 40422 USA
www.BenjaminPress.com
800.765.2139

Text copyright © Patsi B. Trollinger 2012
Illustrations copyright © Benjamin Press 2012
Illustrations by Elizabeth Thompson

ISBN 978-0-9836106-1-8

Printed in Canada

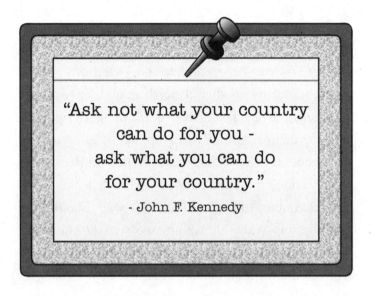

Chapter 1

"Ask not what your country
can do for you -
ask what you can do
for your country."
- John F. Kennedy

Spring break, even when it turns out cold and rainy, has a way of getting my brain headed toward summer. I cornered Keaton to dream about better days filled with sunshine and soccer balls.

"We're gonna beat that bunch from Lexington."

Keaton pumped his fist. "Yeah."

"Sleep till noon every day," I added.

"Uh-huh." Keaton gave me a high-five.

"We'll enjoy ten straight weeks of freedom," I crowed.

We popped knuckles and figured we were the smartest guys in the world.

Boy, were we stupid. The dumbest sixth graders ever born.

The very next day, our town got the big news. One fat headline that spelled our doom. THRILL IN THE 'VILLE: TOWN TO HOST PRESIDENTIAL DEBATE.

At home my mother danced around, waving the newspaper in my face. "Just think of it, Doug. This year the campaign trail will loop and twist across the whole country until it ends up right here in Benville."

At school the next Monday, Ms. Zadecki added political quotes to the WHO SAID IT? wall. She offered bonus points to any kid who memorized the stuff.

Ms. Zadecki kept me in the trouble seat at the front of the room, all because of that little trick with the plastic spiders. Her wall of words was inches away, and those slogans oozed into my brain. I was wise to the fact that sometimes she borrowed fancy phrases from the wall and acted like they belonged to her.

"Today, class," she peered over her glasses, "*you* can do something for *your country*."

She whipped out a stack of star-spangled stationery.

"We're going to write letters to the people in Washington who chose Benville as the first small town to host a presidential debate. We'll thank them for turning the nation's eyes toward Kentucky."

I yawned, and Ms. Zadecki zeroed in on me. "Thank them for giving us an event that will bring hundreds of news crews to our town. *Maybe even ESPN.*" That caused me to sit up straight and start writing.

Zadecki tricked me into writing that letter. One nanosecond later, she was spouting a list of homework assignments. "Special activities," she called them, "to utilize this once-in-a-lifetime opportunity." Then she translated. More writing. More posters. More reading.

Ms. Zadecki had big plans for the last few months of school. And according to her, the minute we arrived back from summer break, we could expect homework stacked up to our eyeballs.

A depressing thought. I tried to erase it from my mind when I caught up with Keaton after the last bell rang. Wouldn't you know? Now that spring break was over, the sun had come out. We cleared the school doors, whooping and kicking an ancient set of hacky-sack balls.

The principal thinks Keaton is way too nice to be my best friend, and he eyed us as we left. We weren't hard to spot, even in that mob of kids. Keaton's dark hair and face were sticking up above everyone else. My blond hair was probably shining like a ship from outer space.

My best friend and I don't look alike, but we agree on how to walk home. Kick a while, run a while. Whoop a little, kick some more. It was perfect until we took our usual shortcut. Then—bam!—the sign practically knocked us down. NO TRESPASSING: CONSTRUCTION UNDERWAY.

And in smaller letters. FUTURE SITE OF MEDIA VILLAGE—SHELBY COLLEGE WELCOMES THE DEBATE.

We were standing at the edge of the world's best soccer field. It belonged to Shelby College, and I guess they thought of the place as a crummy old practice field. To Keaton and me, it was the good-luck site of our summer soccer league. Looked like bad luck had arrived to take over. Guys were scrambling around a truck and a huge pole—the kind that holds power lines.

The truck motor revved and a giant drill on the back began to bore a hole. The drill went right through the grass on the midfield stripe. Dirt flew out of the hole as the drill went deeper and deeper.

Keaton and I were still frozen at the edge of the field when the drill came out and a pole thudded in.

Let me tell you something important. Along every Campaign Trail, there is roadkill. People who get trampled in the political stampede. From the minute that pole hit the ground, hoof beats were headed my way.

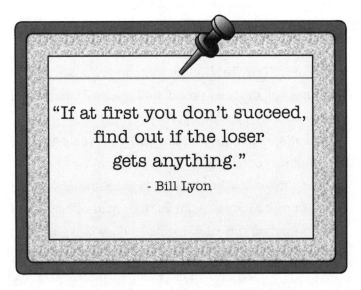

Chapter 2

"If at first you don't succeed,
find out if the loser
gets anything."
- Bill Lyon

My mother could have warned me. Media is her middle name. At least it's the middle name of her job. Director of Media Relations for Shelby College. A fancy way of saying that my mother writes news releases. She calls TV stations and begs them to come to campus. And she puts flashy headlines on the college website every time a student wins some measly award.

If there was going to be a Media Village at the college, you could bet my mother was in on it. The minute she came in the door that night, I demanded some answers. "Why didn't you tell me?"

"Tell you what?" She frowned.

"About the soccer field. They're destroying it to make some kind of village."

Mom sighed, but not like she was sorry about the soccer field. More like she was sorry that I was asking questions. "They're building a temporary power station to support all the news production trucks. The field will be restored after the debate."

"That's six months away," I yelled. "What about the summer soccer league?"

She shoved her briefcase into a chair and ignored me. I stomped to my room, but the smell of barbecued chicken pulled me back to the kitchen a while later. During dinner, Mom hit me with more bad news.

"I'll be working longer hours to prepare for the debate," she said. "I'm not sure you're ready to spend that much time on your own. I've decided to hire a college student two nights a week."

I mashed a pile of peas and muttered in the direction of the green glob. "This debate stuff is ruining my life."

"Oh, come on, Doug." She glared at the glob. "Don't exaggerate. Frankly, I'm surprised you're complaining. The more hours I work now, the more vacation time I'll get later. That could help us take a ski trip next winter."

My mother would make a good boxer. She knows how to hit where it hurts. Still, I wasn't giving up. "I'm too old for a babysitter."

She put on her victory smile, the one that makes me nervous. "That's why I'm hiring a *tutor*."

My only hope was to stall.

"Guess it'll take a while to find a tutor, huh?"

My mother chewed efficiently. "The perfect Shelby student dropped by my office this morning. He can be at our house every Tuesday and Thursday, starting tomorrow. I'll run home from work to introduce the two of you."

I remembered plenty of other college students my mom had hired in the past. A big dumb guy who'd scavenged through the fridge, upset because he couldn't find a beer. A snot-head fellow who stayed on the phone for two hours planning a fraternity party. A girl who insisted on reading Mother Goose rhymes to me.

My mom had predicted each one would be perfect. And what did she say about the tutor? "I promise, Doug. You're going to think he's terrific."

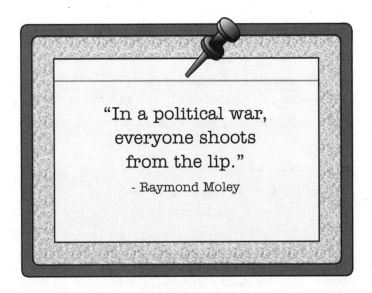

Chapter 3

"In a political war,
everyone shoots
from the lip."

- Raymond Moley

When I met the tutor, I realized that even my worst fears showed a lack of imagination.

Herb Mumpower was round. "Portly," my mother said later. She did not comment on the three hairs on his upper lip that were supposed to be a moustache. Or the white socks.

White socks usually send my mother into a frenzy, but she was dazzled by Herb's efficiency. He whipped a little green notebook out of his pocket and took notes as my mother talked. Rules. Meals. Study time. The nerd wrote down everything. Herb was going to be trouble.

By the time my mother backed her car out of the driveway, I had a plan.

"Think you could help me with some soccer practice?" I asked. "You know—a few kicks on goal." Ha! This guy had probably never seen a soccer ball.

The nerd checked his watch. "Fifteen minutes, max. Then we'll eat a sandwich and hit the books." He was clueless.

I grinned and thought, *I'm gonna clobber you.* In my best imitation of a Boy Scout voice I said: "One on one. You wanna be goalie?"

"Sure."

I should've known when he assumed the goalie stance. Even in khaki pants and a dress shirt, the nerd bent his knees at the perfect angle, got his arms up and ready. I should've focused on those clues right away, but I let my mind wander when I realized someone was watching us. There was a flash of color in a backyard across the way, and I knew we had an audience.

It wouldn't be fair to humiliate the college guy, I figured, so I made my first shot a soft one, about two feet off the ground. Herb caught it easy. That was okay, but he should've known better than to roll the ball back to me instead of punting. Did he think I was some kind of wimp?

Herb wanted to talk while we played. "So, what do you think about the debate coming to Benville? Great learning experience, huh?"

"I hate politics," I announced as the ball rolled toward me. To make myself clear, I yelled as I booted the ball back toward the goal: "This one is for the Republicans."

Herb rolled the ball again. I charged forward and bellowed, "This one is for the Democrats." I kicked with every ounce of power. The sound was incredible when the ball connected with Herb's hands. Thwack!

A perfect save. The guy had suckered me. He had come to our house disguised as a nerdy tutor, and he really was some kind of soccer star.

"Your turn to kick," I called out. Maybe he'd been lucky in the goal.

Herb trotted out of the goal and tossed the ball in my direction. As he headed toward the far end of the yard, he called over one shoulder, "How about a little punt for all the wacko independents?"

I would show him a thing or two about punts.

I booted the ball in a high arc to the end of the yard. Herb scrambled after it, and I got into my goalie stance.

Watching him work the ball back up the yard, I could see that the guy was smooth. Steady dribbling, good control. And fast for somebody who was wide in the middle. He looked like a cannonball coming my way.

All those fine moves got me revved up, and that "gotta win" feeling crept under my skin. Keaton says I go insane when I see someone else excel at soccer. He says it's a flaw in my character.

Flaw, schmaw. I'm just a competitive guy. A guy who could stop anything from this college show-off.

Herb came within shooting range. "Come on," I screamed. "Shoot!"

Boy, did he ever! I saw his foot connect, heard the sizzle of air as the ball streamed toward me inches off the ground. I lunged, felt the ball burn the tips of my fingers. It whammed into my shins, and I gasped. But I had control of the ball.

I got a save. Herb didn't get a goal.

He stood over me. The coldness in his voice shocked me. "Maybe you should've let that go. You aren't wearing shin guards."

It was true. My shins started turning a deep shade of red. The right one was practically glowing. I leaned closer. What were those marks? It was the imprint of the soccer ball, a perfect copy of every line and angle that had blasted my leg. What a powerful kick! And I had stopped it.

Herb looked at his watch and motioned toward the back door. Not a word about the pain in my legs. The guy was a robot. A heartless machine. I tried not to limp as I followed him into the house.

The robot did insist on fixing an ice pack for my shins. Herb made me sit at the kitchen table with the ice while he gathered stuff for sandwiches.

The only problem was that I wanted those lines to stay blasted into my legs to impress Keaton at school. So when Herb looked toward me, the ice pack was on. When Herb turned away, the ice pack was off. I had to preserve the evidence of my incredible save.

Herb spied the little TV that my mom kept in the kitchen. "Mind if we watch the news while we eat?" He was already fiddling with the remote.

A voice thundered from the TV. "Sonny Billings was elected to represent the people of Central Kentucky, and what has he done with your trust?"

Watching the news was bad. Campaign ads were worse. A giant hand appeared on the screen, slamming down a rubber stamp. *Blam!* The hand dissolved into a terrible photo of Billings with two words over it. HIGHER TAXES.

Then the hand again. *Blam!* SCHOOL CLOSINGS. I flinched. Herb was smiling.

Blam! The voice thundered again. "What has Sonny Billings done for you?"

"Billings must be pretty stupid," I said, waving toward the screen, "to pay for an ad like that."

"He didn't," Herb said, eyes still glued to the screen. Then he turned and saw the blank expression on my face. "Somebody else bought the ad—somebody who wants to throw the guy out of office."

"You mean the people who are *against* Billings paid for the ad to make him look bad? That's dumb."

Herb smirked. "Are you kidding? Attack ads work like a charm."

I must've looked like I didn't believe him, because Herb pushed his face closer to mine. "Oh, come on, Doug. You go into attack mode for a soccer game, don't you?"

I didn't answer, and Herb's smirk changed to an evil grin. "Yeah, you've got that competitive streak. Who knows—maybe you'll run for office someday."

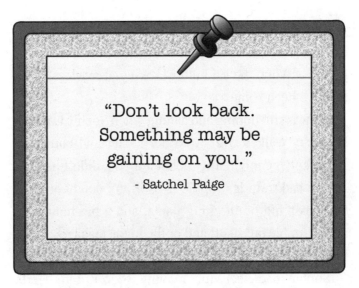

Chapter 4

"Don't look back.
Something may be
gaining on you."

- Satchel Paige

My only hope, I figured, was the bruised shins. The perfect thing to convince my mother that the tutor-nerd was dangerous.

Herb beat me to the draw. Told my mother his version of things the minute she walked in the door.

"Doug insisted we play a little soccer," he said with that robotic smile. "I'm afraid he got carried away. He has some bruises on his shins, but I iced them. Should be fine by tomorrow."

Just like that, Herb put the blame on me and kept the credit for himself.

My mother was blind to the truth. Blinded by his stiff smile and the little green notebook. In her eyes, Herb was perfect.

I was stuck with the guy.

Keaton made me feel better the next morning at school. "Wow," he said after looking at my leg. "That must've been some kick."

He was still oohing and aahing when Sophie Latture-Potensky walked over from her locker and butted in. "That college guy really clobbered you, didn't he?"

The sad truth is, Sophie lives in my neighborhood. She has a big brain, a big name, and a big mouth. In class, Sophie talks soft and polite to the teachers. In the hall she has a voice like a foghorn.

Sophie had seen me playing soccer with Herb, and she'd decided to announce her version of things. In an instant, Tommy Kivacca had his face in mine. "Somebody clobbered the perfect goalie?"

"Nobody clobbered me," I said. "I was supposed to be practicing soft shots with this college guy when, out of nowhere, he decided to kick a zinger. I wasn't wearing shin guards, but I stopped the shot anyway." I pointed to my leg. "There's the evidence. The guy didn't get a goal."

Sophie made a big show of turning away. She called over her shoulder, "Maybe he wouldn't have kicked it so hard if you hadn't been screaming those insults."

Tommy howled with laughter as he walked away, and a few other guys snickered. I slammed my locker shut and turned away just as the second bell rang. I had to run to make it to science class.

Turned out we were building models of the solar system, and guess who was assigned to be my partner. Sophie. She started shuffling through the foam balls on the lab table, chose one to be the sun, and immediately started bugging me.

"I guess your mom hired that college student to keep you out of trouble. I bet you'll be stuck with him for the whole summer."

One of the biggest foam balls on the table—was it Saturn or Jupiter?—would've fit in her mouth. I was sure of it. But the important thing was to stay calm. I coolly reached for one of the smaller planets and a piece of wire.

Sophie glanced at my hands. "Don't you think we should wait to attach Neptune later? It's the farthest planet from the sun." Sophie gave me a look. "And if you happen to be thinking about Pluto, please keep it to yourself."

I lowered the planet back to the table and decided not to say anything about Pluto *or* Sophie.

She continued to needle me. "What you need is a good summer job."

"I don't have time for a job," I said, stabbing a piece of wire into a foam ball. "I have plans."

"Plans?" A pit bull could've barked the word with more respect. "Let me guess. You *plan* to sleep twelve hours a day and mindlessly play soccer the rest of the time."

Sophie inspected me like I was a nest of head lice. "Wake up, Doug, and look around. I have a babysitting job. Keaton mows yards. Tommy works for his father. You are the only person in the entire middle school who plans to do nothing for the summer. Face it—you deserve to have a college student running your life."

She grabbed the last planet out of my hand and popped it into place.

"Oh yeah? Well maybe this little solar system deserves to be hit by an asteroid." I curled one hand into a fist and leaned close to the lab table.

Sophie grabbed the flimsy solar system and raced to the front of the room. Just as she plunked the mess of balls and wires on the teacher's desk, the first bell rang. I was out the door quicker than you could say *summer disaster*.

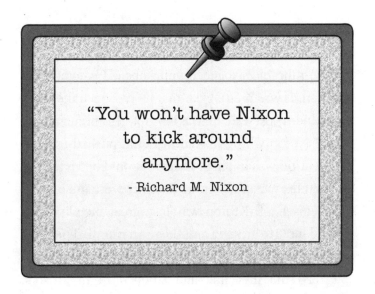

Chapter 5

"You won't have Nixon
to kick around
anymore."

- Richard M. Nixon

Outside the science room, I was nearly creamed by a kid weaving down the hall at top speed. He skidded to a stop beside me and grinned.

I'd seen him before—a new guy, sort of short. The kind of kid who has to keep an eye out for hulks like Tommy Kivacca.

I glanced down the hall. Sure enough, one of Tommy's caveman friends was bearing down on us. He looked as if he'd swallowed a bulldozer for breakfast. Why was that little guy smiling?

When the big guy charged, the short kid did a smooth side step. The dozer tumbled into the science room and crashed into a desk.

There was plenty of time for the short guy and me to bolt toward our lockers. He flashed a thumbs-up.

When the kid's locker swung open, I caught sight of a sign. It was pretty clear that he'd swiped the thing from Zadecki's wall. It was a quote from somebody named Nixon who got tired of being pushed around. The new kid was hoping for inspiration. I had a feeling his troubles weren't over, and neither were mine.

After school, Keaton was in a great mood, which bugged me. He grinned and shoved a rumpled piece of paper into my hand. "Did you see this?"

I read the first line and stopped in my tracks. *SUMMER SOCCER. Benville Middle School players are invited to tryouts at city park, June 8, 6-7 p.m. Coaching staff to be announced.*

Okay, it was good that summer soccer hadn't been canceled because of the debate. But the city park? Bad. The field there was full of rocks. After a hard rain, the goalie box looked like a muddy swimming pool.

Keaton knew what I was thinking. He nudged me. "Hey, we could play on the moon if we had to."

I grinned. "Sure could." I smacked Keaton a high-five and said real fast, "Race you to the hotspot." Then I was off.

It was a tradition. We raced from school all the way to the soccer goal in Keaton's backyard. A mile and a half. The first guy to touch the goal had to promise to buy the loser a milkshake at the Dairy King.

It was hard to say who was really the fastest. Stoplights always slowed us down. Still, I'd bought Keaton a lot of milkshakes in the last year.

My mom swears that all guys stay small until they get to high school. No height and no muscles until ninth grade. It's a rule. But Keaton's body didn't know the rule. He'd grown four inches in the past year, and his legs were super long. It bugged me when I had to buy him a milkshake.

I was still trying to catch up with Keaton when we turned the corner onto Tenth Street. He skidded to a stop, and I thought I might have a chance. But I stopped, too, when I saw what had grabbed his attention. Two men were on the sidewalk down toward the end of the block. They wore black pants, shiny shoes, and dark glasses.

"Look," Keaton whispered to me. "G-men scouting the neighborhood."

I grinned. "You mean *agents*, don't you?"

Every kid at school had heard that Secret Service guys were coming to town. It would've been nice if Keaton and I had been the first to see them, but Tommy Kivacca had beat us. He rolled into school one morning bragging that he and his dad had run into three G-men somewhere downtown. The men had given Tommy a pin with red, white, and blue stripes. He made sure everybody saw the thing.

Sophie had butted into his bragging. "When are you going to get this straight? The term *G-man* refers to someone who works for the FBI. The officers who have recently come to Benville are with the U.S. Secret Service. They are *agents*."

Agents. G-men. Who cared what you called them when you got to see them up close. In your own neighborhood.

Keaton whispered, "My dad says the Secret Service has to check out all the streets around the college. They're making sure everything is safe for the candidates."

At least Tommy had been telling the truth about what they wear. According to him, agents don't wear police uniforms. They like to blend in with the local scenery while looking for stuff that might be suspicious.

To hear Tommy tell it, these guys have a long list of worries. Everything from clunky potholes (don't want to damage a limousine) to weird people (it's not nice to scream at the candidates).

The agents could find a lot to bother them on Tenth Street. A pothole the size of Montana. And plenty of weird-thinking people. There was Sophie's dad, who carved rocks. Their ancient neighbor who had flags that weren't red, white, and blue. And a new couple down at the corner who kept a statue of a warthog in their flower garden.

Yep, those agents would be busy on Tenth Street. But somebody should've told them that in Benville, you don't blend in by wearing black pants and shiny shoes on a warm day.

At home that night, my mother wasn't impressed by my report.

"Secret Service guys—oh, sure," she said, like it happened every day. "Probably the same agents I talked to this morning. There was a meeting on campus to talk about security for the debate."

"You *talked* to them?" I sucked in a deep breath and tried not to yell. "Did you get me one of those pins or something cool?"

She looked at me like I'd asked her to eat worms. "Oh, Doug, it would've been unprofessional to ask for a souvenir in the middle of a meeting."

Then she softened up. "Sorry. I didn't know you wanted one."

She patted my hand like I was three years old, and that's when I made a decision. "I'm thinking about getting a summer job," I said.

"A job?"

"Yeah. Thought I'd ask around the neighborhood—see if I can find something."

"Well, it's fine for you to look, but don't get your hopes up." She hesitated. "I've already talked to Herb about continuing through the summer."

She ignored the explosion on my side of the table and went on. "Herb had hoped to get a job with a political campaign, but so far that hasn't worked out. Really, Doug, he'll be such a good influence on you. This will be a perfect arrangement for all of us."

"Yeah," I muttered. "A perfect disaster."

I unloaded my problems on Keaton at our lockers the next morning. "Can you believe it? I'm stuck with the tutor-guy for the whole summer."

"Maybe it won't be so bad." Keaton was ready with some stupid *be happy* advice. "Maybe he'll practice soccer with you."

Not so bad? Hah!

The next Tuesday, Herb came to our house. He tutored me in math and then made me stuff envelopes for a political mailing. On Thursday, we had thirty minutes of science homework, two minutes of soccer, and an hour watching some political show on TV. Every week was the same: homework and politics.

With Zadecki for homework and Herb for company, my life was a wreck. It stayed that way until the community barbecue the Saturday before Memorial Day.

I could smell the food the minute I followed my mom into the big building at the county fairgrounds. Barbecue, baked beans, homemade cakes and pies. The only thing in my way was the huge crowd of people handing out political buttons and flyers.

I was prepared to push my way to the food line, but my mom—who had our tickets—froze in her tracks.

There she was, in the middle of all that political stuff, and she was supposed to keep her mouth shut. She'd said it herself. "The one bad thing about the debate is that college employees have to be neutral. We're the host site, and I have to act nice to everybody. No mouthing off in public."

My mother loves a good political argument the way I love booting a soccer ball. She calls Uncle Zeke up in Cincinnati and rags on the Republicans, just to get him fired up. She sends e-mails to Aunt Lana in St. Louis with tirades about the Democrats. My mother says her family is all mixed up politically, and she loves it that way. More opportunities to argue.

At the barbecue, we were surrounded by people ready and willing to argue. My mom couldn't say a word. Her face was twitching, and she looked miserable. As things turned out, she also was dangerous.

Mom was willing to overlook Sophie's dad in the corner with his Save the Whales bumper stickers. And the warthog man parading around wearing some kind of weird old Army hat. But when Mom caught sight of a big sign on the wall, she let out a low growl. The sign said TRIUMPH WITH TREADWAY. In front of it, Tommy Kivacca's dad was handing out political buttons. Mom muttered, "Ooh, I'd like to get my hands on that man."

I grabbed her arm and started toward the food line. "Let's eat. I'm starving."

My mom followed me, her mouth pinched together, and she grabbed the food she wanted. Barbecue and cole slaw. A bowl of that weird-looking stew called burgoo. Usually she tries to make me take a bowl and tells me that burgoo is a Kentucky classic. For once, she was quiet.

Our trays were loaded, and we were almost to a table when Herb, the tutor-nerd, turned up. "Nice to see you, Ms. Alverton," he said. The three-hair moustache quivered. My mother stared at something on his shirt.

"A Treadway button?" she said, not loud but plenty sharp.

"Yes," he answered in that chilly robot voice. "Mr. Kivacca hired me to help with a local campaign." Herb was gripping a new notebook. Blue.

Next thing I knew, Mr. Kivacca had barged into the conversation. He gave my mom a fake smile. "I see that you know this talented young man." Mr. Kivacca clapped Herb on the back and then patted his own jacket, which was loaded with Treadway buttons. "Herb is going to help me get the right man in office."

My mother's tray started to quiver. "How can you support a candidate who's willing to wreck the state education budget?"

Mr. Kivacca's smile disappeared. Score one for my mom, I thought. Then I remembered. She wasn't supposed to be discussing politics in public. I nudged her arm. I might hate my mom's job, but I didn't want her to get fired.

"It's short-sighted," she went on. "Irresponsible."

I nudged her again. And, listen, I swear it was a gentle nudge. The thing that happened next was entirely my mother's fault.

She tried to shift her tray, and the burgoo started to slide. Just a tiny slide until my mother jerked the tray. That's when all the food got going. Burgoo, barbecue, cole slaw. Everything hopped off the tray and sailed through the air. It reminded me of a perfect crossing kick—the kind that puts a soccer ball right on target for the net.

But there wasn't any net. Just a couple of very surprised guys who had come to the picnic wearing political buttons and were going to leave wearing a buffet.

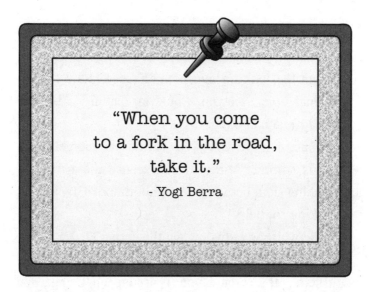

Chapter 6

"When you come
to a fork in the road,
take it."

- Yogi Berra

Maybe Herb quit. Or maybe my mother fired him. I can't say for sure, but quicker than you can say *burgoo*, the tutor was out of my life.

At least I thought so. By the morning of Memorial Day, I was feeling free. My mother might track down another student, but at least I would have one whole day with no school and no problems.

Make that half a day.

Our neighborhood had a picnic that afternoon, and I caught sight of my mom yakking with a bunch of women near the dessert table. When she was in a group like that, it usually spelled trouble for me. The last time a bunch of moms got in a huddle, they decided that no kid should have a cell phone until he got to high school. It was like they could pass a law at one of these picnics.

From the look on my mom's face, I had a feeling they had done it again. She was making a beeline toward Keaton and me.

"Doug, I hope you were serious about getting a job this summer," she said. "Because there may be something right here in the neighborhood. Mrs. Bering is looking for help."

"The warthog lady down at the corner?"

Keaton snickered, and my mother gave both of us a cold stare. "It's a boar, Doug. That statue in their garden is a wild boar. It's the logo for the Berings' business." Keaton and I doubled over with laughter.

My mother leaned closer and folded her arms. "Too bad you're not interested. I'll get on the phone tonight and start looking for a replacement for Herb."

I snapped to attention. "What kind of job?"

"She needs help delivering merchandise. Muscle work, she called it."

The deal was sounding better. "Right up my alley," I announced.

Keaton elbowed into the conversation. "Do you think she'd hire both of us?"

By dinnertime that night, we had a deal. Keaton and I would work three hours a day for the warthog enterprise, the only business in our neighborhood. Keaton's mom would feed us lunch. The rest of the time, my mother was willing to let me be a free man.

When Keaton and I reported for work a week later, Mr. Bering answered the door. A skinny guy with white hair. He had a newspaper in one hand and a cup of coffee in the other. His voice came out like a snarl.

"Follow me, boys," he growled. "It's time to get to work."

It took us a while to go down the steps to the basement because Mr. Bering had something wrong with his foot. When we finally got to the bottom, he swept the air with one hand. "Welcome to the land of the free and the brave—and the freebie." He made a sound that might have been a laugh, then settled into a chair beside the steps and unfolded his newspaper.

The basement looked like a cross between Ms. Zadecki's class and Louie's Pawn Shop down on East Main. The walls were covered with slogans, and several tables were loaded with junk. Every inch of the floor was piled high with boxes.

On a table close to Mrs. Bering, I saw rows and rows of bobbleheads. I figured they were football hulks or baseball sluggers. Turned out to be presidents. Bill Clinton and Ronald Reagan were standing side-by-side with fat plastic heads on skinny little bodies. George Bush and John Kennedy were there, too.

I knew my presidents pretty well. Mom had bought a set of plastic placemats covered with their pictures, and I was always wiping spaghetti sauce off Reagan or Kennedy or somebody. I had their names memorized by the time I got to fourth grade.

The presidents had a good time on my placemat. Maybe they liked being bobbleheads, too. Mrs. Bering was packing them, in sets of four, into white boxes stamped with gold letters. *Izzo Communications: Head and shoulders above the competition.*

Another table was piled high with little Statue of Liberty figures. Keaton squeezed Lady Liberty's toe, and her torch threw out a light. The book in her hand carried a message. *Haverty's Lamp Shop: We light up your life.*

One wall was nearly covered by a poster of a plastic purple warthog with words scrawled across its back. *Bering's Specialty Advertising—No business is boring with a slogan from Bering.*

If Mrs. Bering didn't want to look like the warthog on the wall, she shouldn't have been wearing that purple shirt and slacks. She wasn't a small person. And her cell phone with a headset? Well, the microphone looked a lot like a tusk.

I'll say one thing. Mrs. Bering was the most cheerful warthog I'd ever met.

"Don't you love those Lady Liberty flashlights?" she asked. "Help yourself—we have plenty." Before I had time to grab a handful, she pointed to a stack of cartons near a side door. "We're ready to load up for deliveries."

Keaton and I jammed six big boxes into Mrs. Bering's van. After a quick delivery to the lamp store, she drove to the ice cream shop on Main Street. The owner went wild when Keaton and I pried open a carton for her to inspect. She hoisted a stack of cheap plastic bowls.

"Fabulous," she gushed. "The bowls look like Uncle Sam hats, turned upside down. Let's try them out."

Mrs. Bering laughed. "Good idea. I have some expert taste-testers with me."

"It's a new flavor in honor of the debate," the woman told Keaton and me as she scooped ice cream. "Luscious Liberty. We took our premium vanilla blend and added lots of blueberries and strawberries. If we serve it in these bowls—presto—we have the Liberty Bowl Special."

She handed Keaton and me two bowls piled high with ice cream, topped with a dollop of whipped cream, a maraschino cherry, and a tiny plastic flag.

Whoa, that stuff was good.

As the last bite of Liberty slid down my throat, Mrs. Bering motioned us toward the door. "Glad you like the bowls," she called to the owner. "I'll talk with the boys about the other promotional idea."

In the van, Mrs. Bering asked if Keaton or I might be able to work at the ice cream shop that afternoon. I was relieved when Keaton said he had a mowing job. There probably was more ice cream to sample, and I wanted it all to myself.

Things sounded even better when Mrs. Bering said I would earn twenty dollars for three hours of work. She didn't mention the costume until I met her back at the ice cream shop after lunch. That's when she and the shop owner hauled out a pair of red and white striped pants plus a white jacket with blue stars. Big hat, too, and a fake beard that looked like a clump of ragged cotton balls.

I stumbled into the men's room and put on the costume. When I came out and Mrs. Bering aimed at my chin with the cotton balls and a dab of glue, I had second thoughts. The owner upped her offer. "Twenty-five dollars. It's a great opportunity."

That's how I ended up parading back and forth on the sidewalk beside Main Street. My job was to persuade everybody in sight to try the most exciting new flavor of ice cream in Benville.

"Get your Liberty Bowl," I called to a man who came out of the bank next door. He ignored me. I turned up the volume of cheerfulness. "Come on, folks, try the Liberty Bowl special."

Maybe the volume was a little too much. I heard a kid crying on the sidewalk behind me.

I turned around, and who did I see? Sophie Latture-Potensky, taking care of two little kids, the Zirnheld twins. Knee-high maniacs, from what I'd heard.

The boy twin was bawling, feet planted on the sidewalk. "I want to go home." The girl twin was yanking Sophie toward the ice cream shop. "Ice cream!" she shouted and glared at her brother.

I knew that look. The girl was getting ready to kick her brother, and Sophie was clueless. The little guy would get mauled.

"Guess what?" I said, moving closer to the twins. "You could be the first kids in town to own a Liberty Bowl." A trickle of sweat slid down my arm.

The girl stopped her foot in midair, and the boy's bawling changed to a snuffle. "Red, white and blue," I whispered, like it was the world's biggest secret.

Suddenly both twins bolted toward the shop. Sophie ran to catch up with them.

That was my first success of the day. Pretty soon, I knew I had a natural flair for advertising. In the first hour, seventeen people went in to buy ice cream. In the second hour, twenty-four. By that time, the trickle of sweat inside my jacket had changed to a river. Then Tommy Kivacca showed up.

"Well, look who's in his Halloween costume. Isn't it a little early for trick-or-treating, Dougie Wuggie?"

Some customers coming out of the ice cream shop steered around the two of us.

"I'm gonna trick-or-treat you," I growled softly. "Back off."

Tommy sneered. "Oh, wow, maybe Uncle Sam has an attitude."

Sweat poured down my legs, turning the red stripes to maroon. The costume was going to make it hard for me to land a good punch.

"Excuse me, boys." A woman who was headed into the ice cream shop lowered her sunglasses to look at us. "Is there some kind of problem here?"

That was enough to get Tommy off my case and into the ice cream shop. On his way out, he managed to flick a glop of Luscious Liberty in my direction. As it melted, chunks of blueberry and strawberry slid down the striped pants.

When the store owner saw the stains at the end of the day, she kept the extra five dollars she'd promised. "Cleaning bill," she said abruptly. "It was your responsibility to keep the suit in its original condition."

This job thing is a rip-off, I told myself as I walked home. Then my hand rustled through the money in my pocket. A crisp ten from Mrs. Bering for the morning, and two more from the ice cream store for the afternoon.

I thought the debate stuff would be nothing but a bunch of windbag politicians. Nobody had mentioned that it might be profitable.

At home, I emptied my pockets and glanced in the mirror. One little tuft of Uncle Sam's beard was still stuck to my chin. It took an hour to scrub it off before I headed for soccer tryouts.

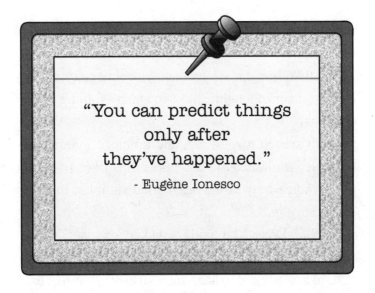

Chapter 7

"You can predict things
only after
they've happened."
- Eugène Ionesco

I was determined to be the first person to arrive at tryouts. No way I'd wait for Keaton to get home from his mowing job. I got on my bike thirty minutes early and pedaled like crazy all the way to the park. I hit the field running, ready to warm up with some of my favorite drills. Hadn't been at it more than five minutes when things started to go sour.

Who else arrived early? Tommy Kivacca.

And two steps behind him? His father.

Mr. Kivacca has a history of hanging around tryouts to pester the coaches about his son. No surprise that he was there, but the person behind him was a shocker. None other than Herb, the tutor-nerd, wearing shorts, a T-shirt, and cleats. His legs were six shades whiter than snow.

My first thought: a snowman with shin guards.

My second thought: that snowman is going to be our coach!

Herb started toward me, and up close I could see the hairs trembling on his upper lip. Four of them now. Maybe he was having a good summer, in spite of the burgoo.

"Hello, Doug," he said. "Glad to see you." Herb offered a hand for me to shake, but his arm was kind of stiff, like he wanted to keep some distance between us.

I heard Tommy snickering. "Yeah, Doug, it's great to have you here. I just wish you'd worn that cute little Uncle Sam costume."

Tommy is a spoiled brat. Every summer, his dad paid him to loaf around the Kivacca Printing Company. He'd probably done nothing all day except stuff his face with Twinkies.

And another thing about Tommy? He's a goalie-wannabe. A guy who says he wants to be a goalie, but never quite comes through. With his size—not to mention that mouth—he could be a good one. Except he never wants to move. Not at all. The way Tommy figures things, if he stands in the box scowling, he ought to be able to scare the opposing team.

Maybe that worked back in third grade, when Tommy was as big as the goal. Those days were over. Our goals were wider, and a good player could place a ball in any corner. The goalie would have to be willing to kill himself diving for a save. Tommy wouldn't dive for anything except Twinkies.

His father, on the other hand, was more than a wannabe. Mr. Kivacca had enough money to sponsor ten soccer teams if he wanted to. Any idiot could see that he'd agreed to sponsor *this* team in hopes his son would be the goalie. He'd found a coach who would do things the Kivacca way.

I cleared my throat and spoke to Herb in my most polite voice. "Are you going to be our coach?"

Mr. Kivacca stepped forward and draped an arm across Herb's shoulder, sort of like he owned him. "Yes," Mr. Kivacca boomed. "Herb Mumpower is our man of the hour. The perfect coach for the Thrill from the 'Ville."

Even without the rhymes, it would've been enough to make me gag.

Herb's face pinched together for just a second, like he was in pain. Then he was all business. He actually whipped out a notebook (this one was red) and glanced at his watch. "We'd better get started. Looks like some other fellows are rolling in."

Six guys were trotting toward us. Keaton was in the middle, waving to me. When he broke from the group and headed my way, a short guy followed him. It was the kid I'd seen at school with the sign in his locker.

Keaton gave me a high-five and turned to the little guy. "Doug, this is Nick Stone. Trying out for midfielder, and he's the fastest kid in school. He transferred into Benville too late to play for the school team last year. This summer, he's our secret weapon."

Keaton's like that—always encouraging people. I figured the kid had to be fast just to stay alive in middle school. But a secret weapon? The guy barely came up to my armpit. Still, I remembered my manners. "Good luck, Nixon," I said, whacking him on the back.

He gave me a funny look. "Nick," he said. "My name's Nick."

"Right," I said. But a few minutes later, when I called him Nixon again, the kid cracked up. "Okay, okay," he said. "But don't tell Ms. Zadecki about the poster I swiped from her wall."

"Sure." We sealed the deal with a knuckle-bump.

Tryouts got underway, and Herb put Tommy in the goal. The nerd-coach scribbled in his notebook while we ran shooting drills. Nixon shoved balls past Tommy faster than a popgun, and I laughed.

When it was my turn in the goal, I didn't have time to laugh. The new kid was good. I was gasping for breath when Herb called us to the sideline.

"I want to thank you for trying out," he said as we flopped on the ground around him. He glanced at his notebook before he went on. "I'm pleased to tell you that everyone will have a spot on the team. Our sponsor, Mr. Kivacca, has plenty of uniforms."

Herb cleared his throat. "Uh...now Mr. Kivacca has a few announcements to make."

"Boys." Mr. Kivacca sounded like he was starting a sermon. "You have a special opportunity this summer. A once-in-a-lifetime experience."

Uh-oh. I'd heard those words before.

Mr. Kivacca was still talking. "At the same time you're playing a sport you love, you can publicize our town."

Yeah, I thought, *and the Kivacca Printing Company.*

Mr. Kivacca began rummaging in a box he'd hauled to the field from his car. "You can show your love of the United States." His voice kept getting louder. "And you can remind the entire state that Benville is a bastion of democracy."

We had a kid on the team named Jacob Bastien, and a few guys laughed. My eyes were stuck on the thing Mr. Kivacca had pulled from the box. It was a uniform.

The kind of uniform a team wears when it wants to show off instead of play ball.

The shiny blue shorts were covered with wavy white stripes, and the red shirt had white stars thrown across one shoulder. Huge white letters crossed the front of the jersey: KIVACCA'S THRILL FROM THE 'VILLE.

How could this happen to me? If I wanted to play summer soccer, I would have to be coached by Herb and wear a jersey that made it look as if I was actually happy about the stupid debate in Benville. When the guys from Lexington caught sight of those uniforms, they would laugh us off the field.

"What's the deal?" Nixon whispered. "Are we beauty queens or soccer players?"

"Roadkill," I answered.

I nearly barfed during Mr. Kivacca's sermon. Then Herb announced the roster. He read the entire list from his notebook, including the final bombshell.

"Two players will share goalkeeper duties," he said. "Tommy Kivacca and Doug Alverton."

Wait a minute. Herb had listed Kivacca first and me second. Did that mean Tommy would be the starter and I would be the backup? The evil smile on Mr. Kivacca's face gave me a very bad feeling.

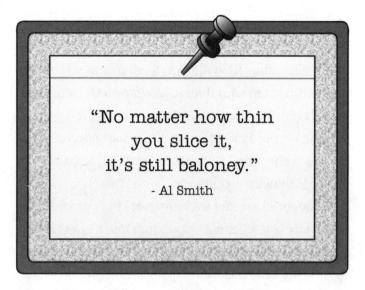

Chapter 8

"No matter how thin
you slice it,
it's still baloney."

- Al Smith

I hated fancy uniforms. I hated sharing the goalie box with Tommy Kivacca. I hated getting up early to go to work. When Keaton and I met at the Berings' house the next morning, I was in one foul mood.

Mrs. Bering was her usual bubbly self.

"Tomorrow's a big day at the college," she said. She was practically fluttering with excitement. "I'll bet Doug's mother has told him all about it."

I shook my head. If my mom had said anything, I had ignored it.

"It's a huge media tour with lots of TV news producers and important people from Washington." Mrs. Bering chattered all the way down the steps to the basement. "The college and the local Chamber of

Commerce want to make a good impression, so they've decided to give each visitor a gift bag."

Unbelievable. Benville was giving presents to the men and women who'd marched into town to ruin the soccer field and wreck my life.

Mrs. Bering held up a blue tote bag covered with red and white stars. "Our job is to fill these bags with classic Kentucky goodies."

I thought she meant trick-or-treat kinds of junk. But let me tell you what was going into those bags. Boxes of melt-in-your-mouth fudge from a candy company up in Frankfort. Baseball caps from the minor-league team in Lexington. Miniature bats from the Louisville Slugger Company.

Good stuff. Keaton and I spent the morning putting it into gift bags for people who didn't deserve it.

When my mother got home from work that evening, I told her exactly what I thought. "Those people from Washington have already taken over the whole town. It's dumb to give them presents, too."

She shot me a warning look. "You need to work on your attitude."

I ignored her warning, determined to get in the last word. "Free country," I muttered.

My mom is way too strict. She says it's because she has to do all the discipline for a mom and a dad. I think that's just an excuse. But for muttering two words, I got two nights without television privileges. Maybe it was a good thing. I spent extra time outside with a soccer ball. At the next team practice, I was fantastic in the goal.

I stopped eight shots during scrimmage, and Herb congratulated me. After practice ended, he stayed at the park to give Keaton and me extra tips.

"You've got great hands," Herb told me. "But you need to work on your legs." He showed me exercises that would improve my leaping ability. Knee bends, cat springs, side thrusts. Then, for another half hour, Herb and Keaton kicked shots that had me jumping straight up, sideways, and backwards.

It wasn't because Herb liked Keaton or me. What he liked was winning.

With Tommy in the goal, our team was looking like a bunch of losers. Tommy was plenty strong, but he had a tiny brain attached to a very big mouth. Herb couldn't get him to understand something basic: yelling at your own teammates was stupid. We didn't exactly get inspired when Tommy yelled stuff like, "Come on, you slowpokes, run faster!"

I figured Herb was getting worried about what Tommy might do in our first game. He didn't have to wonder for long. Two days. Then the Woodford County team rolled into city park, and Mr. Kivacca insisted that Tommy would play goalie.

Herb put me in a defensive position in front of the net. I defended at least ten possible scores from the Woodford Wolverines, but midway through the second half, I let a shot get by me. Tommy barely moved. He watched the ball roll into the net and then shouted at me, "Alverton, you're a moron."

I considered letting the next ball slam right into his midsection.

A few minutes later, Keaton muffed a throw-in, and Tommy screamed, "Idiot." The next time Keaton got the ball, his dribbling looked sort of klutzy.

Tommy couldn't see the truth. If you scream at your own teammates, they can lose their winning edge. Lose the whole game, which is exactly what we did. The Woodford guys chanted as they left the field: "The Thrill from the 'Ville got a chill. The Thrill from the 'Ville got a chill."

I glanced in Herb's direction. His hands were clenched into fists.

During our second game, Nixon cured Tommy's big mouth, pretty much by accident. Nixon missed a pass, and the Stanford team used his mistake to get a score. Nixon felt terrible about it, and what did Tommy do? While the refs were setting up for the kick-off, Tommy charged out to the midfield stripe, shook his fist in the air, and bellowed in Nixon's direction, "You midget, I ought to kill you."

Nixon was ready to fight, and it took half the team to hold him back. But while I was hanging onto his jersey, a miracle happened. The referee handed Tommy a red card.

The field got so quiet I could hear Tommy sputter, "But I was talking to a guy on *my* team. Just trying to encourage him."

The ref's reply came through loud and clear: "What I heard, young man, was a threat. The league has a rule against threatening language. Automatic two-game suspension." The ref hoisted a red card and steered Tommy to the sideline.

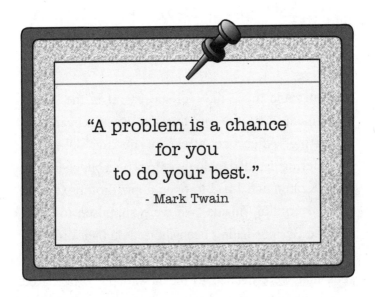

Chapter 9

"A problem is a chance
for you
to do your best."

- Mark Twain

Some coaches would've argued and tried to keep Tommy in the game. Herb barely looked toward the ref. Instead, our coach was waving frantically for me to come to the sideline. In a flash, I was pulling on my goalie shirt and gloves.

Maybe we got pumped. Or maybe the Stanford Strikers were in shock over the weirdest red card in the history of soccer. Somehow we pulled out a victory. The next week, while Tommy was still benched, we did it again.

Herb got excited during that game. He scribbled in his notebook for a while and then tossed the thing on the ground when our team started to come alive.

Keaton scored on a header, and the robot-coach applauded. We whipped the Mercer Marauders with a 4-2 score.

That game made me feel successful in the soccer department. My life on the job wasn't nearly so interesting. After two weeks of making deliveries, Mrs. Bering decided to do inventory on a bunch of new stuff. Keaton and I had to open a gazillion boxes and count everything inside. We were supposed to make sure the Berings hadn't been shorted on their orders.

Keaton and I started with a batch of musical ink pens that were headed to the newspaper office. Red pens with white lettering. *Read the Bugle—Stay in tune with the times.* Click the top, and the pen played the national anthem. A little bumpy, but you knew it was the anthem.

We discovered we could drive Mr. Bering wild by clicking a pen every few seconds. When the bumpy little notes of *Oh say can you see* started grinding out for the tenth time, he shouted at Keaton and me. "Stop playing with the merchandise."

We counted refrigerator magnets for Stevenson's Air Conditioning Repair. *Be cool: Vote this year.* We stacked paperweights for Burke's Bakery that looked like little loaves of bread. *May every good candidate rise to the top.*

The orders rarely ran short. Most of the suppliers sent too much. Just enough to make the numbers weird. One thousand eleven musical ink pens. Seven hundred fifty-six magnets. Four hundred thirty-two paperweights.

That was just in the first hour. By the time we left at noon, we'd counted at least a zillion bumper stickers, rulers, and miniature flags.

Keaton's mom had fixed us homemade pizza for lunch, and I automatically counted the pieces. Eight. Keaton's brother and sisters weren't home, so I figured that meant three slices for me, three for Keaton, and two for his mother. If she was really hungry, she might short my order.

My mother swears that Keaton's parents try to spoil me because I don't have a dad. It's not like I remember having a dad (mine died in a car wreck when I was a baby), but it's fine with me when Mr. Jones takes me to ball games. It's extra-fine the way Mrs. Jones loves to feed me.

"Have some more pizza," she said, offering me one of her slices. I almost took it before I realized that Keaton was giving me the stinkeye.

"No, thanks," I said as I polished off the last bit of pepperoni on my plate. Just in time, because somebody else showed up at the door. It was Sophie, returning a magazine her mother had borrowed.

Keaton's mom started chatting. "How are things at the Latture-Potensky household?"

Sophie mother, Professor Latture, taught at the college. Her dad, Mr. Potensky, was an artist who carved rocks. Sophie used both names, which added up to a mouthful.

Keaton's mom loved keeping up with neighborhood gossip. "Well, Sophie, is it true that your dad has started a new sculpture?"

"The *artist*," Sophie said sarcastically, "is being very secretive. He locks the door to his studio and says he has a commission that requires privacy." She made a face. "He won't even let me take a peek."

"A commission?" Keaton's mother was impressed. "That's good, isn't it—he's guaranteed of a buyer?"

Sophie snorted. "I don't believe him." She turned on her heel to leave. "I think it's just another stupid project he's doing for a friend."

"Oh, Sophie," Keaton's mom followed her onto the porch. "You're way too hard on your father."

Sophie's attitude toward Mr. Potensky wasn't a secret. In second grade, she sold her father to me on career day. Mr. Potensky had arrived wearing torn jeans and sporting a ponytail. A few kids snickered, and that's when Sophie whipped out a quarter and shoved it into my hand. "Here, Doug—you go sit with my dad and his tools. I'll sit with your mom and her briefcase."

I took Sophie's money that day and convinced my mom to make the switch.

It turned out terrific. I got to try my hand at using a mallet and a chisel. I learned to tell the difference between Kentucky limestone and Italian marble. And Mr. Potensky became a neighborhood buddy for Keaton and me.

No matter what Sophie said, I thought her dad was cool. He never complained when we dashed into his studio. Never got mad, even when my mother tried to suck him into a political argument. Never acted embarrassed, even when his daughter was a jerk.

Back in second grade, rock carving had seemed like a great career. But I'd learned that Sophie might be right about the money side of things. I'd seen one of Mr. Potensky's carvings down at city hall with a plaque that said *Donated to the City of Benville.* There was another carving and a plaque over at the college library. If Mr. Potensky kept giving stuff away, he'd never make much money.

Keaton and I eyed each other while Sophie talked to Mrs. Jones. When we headed outside after lunch, we looked toward Mr. Potensky's studio.

"It does seem funny to see his door closed in the middle of the summer," I said to Keaton.

"Yeah," Keaton laughed. "Remember how we used to run in and out of there?"

I shivered to think that we'd played tag with Sophie. But even after Keaton and I started avoiding her, we kept popping into the studio. We'd ask about Mr. Potensky's carving, and he'd ask about soccer. It was part of the neighborhood routine. Until this year.

That night, I asked my mother if she knew anything about Mr. Potensky's new project. "Nah," she said. "Probably just another piece he's donating to the city." She shuttled leftovers from the table to the fridge.

My mother wasn't exactly close friends with Sophie's parents. Mr. Potensky and Professor Latture liked to call themselves old hippies. That drove my mother crazy. My mother is young—she looks like a kid compared to Sophie's parents. And to hear her talk, hippies were worse than nose hair. People who tried to ruin the world before she was born.

That was her opinion of Mr. Potensky. I happened to think the guy was nice.

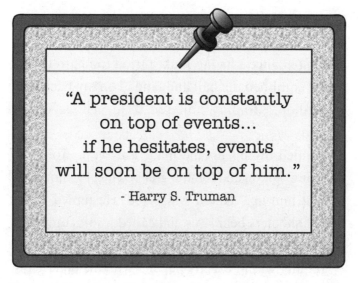

Chapter 10

"A president is constantly on top of events... if he hesitates, events will soon be on top of him."

- Harry S. Truman

If there is a list of humans who are worse than nose hair, Tommy Kivacca's name comes first.

At our next soccer practice, Herb set up a shooting drill and put me in the goal. Tommy immediately started whining. "What about me? I'll be eligible to play this week. You promised I'd get some practice time in the goal."

Herb agreed that Tommy would get a turn, but that didn't cure his attitude. He dragged his feet during shooting drills, slowing down the whole line. When Nixon got a shot past me, Tommy cheered like it was major league soccer.

About the time I was ready to belt Tommy, Mr. Kivacca showed up. He scowled toward the goal and motioned Herb over to talk. In two seconds, Tommy was in the goal, and I was in the shooting line.

First chance I had to kick, I tried too hard to nail him. I squibbed the ball and landed on my backside. "Woo-hoo," Tommy hollered. "Get a load of the bun boy."

I pulled myself up and made a move in Tommy's direction. Nixon and Keaton grabbed me. "I know how to shut him up," Nixon whispered. He turned to the line of shooters behind us and called a soft command. "Double time."

Tommy wasn't exactly popular with the other guys, and suddenly nobody waited between shots. No sooner had Tommy lunged for one ball than another was coming his way. Wham. A ball hit him on the shoulder. Wham. A ball smacked him on the thigh. Wham, wham, wham. Arm, ankle, knee.

Tommy hadn't been hit more than two or three times before he started squealing. "Ow! Ouch! Stop it, you guys!" And the ultimate no-no. He whined to the coach. "Herb, make them quit."

"Cut it out, boys!" Herb shouted. Everyone stopped shooting, but we couldn't stop grinning.

Mr. Kivacca glared at me. "Don't be so hasty, Coach Mumpower," he said loudly. "Doug seems to love this double-time shooting. Let's put him back in the goal."

The guys tried to be considerate, but every time they slowed down, Tommy yelled, "Faster!"

Balls came toward me quicker than spit-wads in the library. Most of the guys tried to keep the kicks easy, but Tommy delivered a fast one that nailed me in the back while I was reaching for another shot.

Man, that hurt. But nobody was going to hear me whine. Not a word.

The next morning, every muscle in my body was screaming. I actually hoped the Berings would let Keaton and me sit around all morning doing inventory. Instead, the warthog man came out to meet us on the sidewalk. He barked out our plan for the day.

"We're going downtown to hang bunting. I'm supposed to make sure you get it right." He motioned us toward the van. "Everything's ready to go."

Mrs. Bering was in the driver's seat. "Morning, fellows," she said as we climbed in.

Mr. Bering slid into the front seat, grumbling. "So we're going to decorate the whole town, are we?"

"Bunting isn't a decoration, honey," Mrs. Bering said cheerfully. "It's an expression of patriotism."

The real story? Bunting is red, white, and blue stuff that can bury an entire town in a matter of minutes. Mrs. Bering had miles and miles of it. Enough to cover the front of the courthouse and the bank. The ice cream shop, the post office, and everything in between.

The Berings had signed a contract with the Chamber of Commerce to cover all those buildings. But only part way. Keaton and I couldn't just grab a mile-long piece of bunting and take off running. No, we would have to hang the stuff in short sections, decorating one window at a time.

Mrs. Bering watched us unload the boxes, and then headed down the street to the bank. Mr. Bering pointed toward the shoe store. "Do it right," he commanded. "Or you'll have to take it down and start over."

While I was perched on the ladder, the hammer slipped out of my hand. A tiny accident, and the hammer didn't even hit the UPS man who was making a delivery. Bering cursed anyway.

Next stop was the jewelry store. That's where I stumbled off the ladder and banged into a plate glass window. Nothing broke—not me or the window—but I guess the noise startled the jeweler. He dropped the diamond he'd been holding with a pair of tweezers. You'd have thought it was a huge inconvenience for him to spend a few minutes on his hands and knees trying to find the thing. He shouted at me through the window. Bering limped inside to calm him down.

When Mr. Bering came out, he muttered something about coffee and headed toward the diner.

With Bering off our backs, Keaton and I got into a rhythm. We'd finished a whole row of windows by the time Mrs. Bering came back. She was admiring our work when a woman tapped her on the shoulder.

"Excuse me, ma'am. We're from WLXK-TV." She motioned to a man with a video camera. "We're putting together a story about Benville's preparations for the debate. Would it be okay if we shot some tape and got an interview with these boys?"

"That would be wonderful," Mrs. Bering gushed. Then she turned to Keaton and me. "Don't be nervous, fellows. Just be yourselves."

I hated to tell Mrs. Bering, but the last time I'd tried to be myself, my mother grounded me.

The camera guy gave orders. "Light's not good. Move left."

Keaton and I shifted our ladders. "Back up," the man ordered. "Turn at an angle. Can you wipe that dirt off the ladder?" We got bossed around until the camera guy was satisfied.

"Turn your face toward the camera," he told us. "Tuck in your shirt. Stretch your arms. And smile."

Keaton and I stood on the ladders, twisted like pretzels, with stupid smiles pasted on our faces. Even before the camera started rolling, we had an audience. Every nosy person on Main Street gathered around us and the reporter. Sophie was there, with the Zirnheld twins tugging on her arms.

The reporter jotted down our names and finally started asking questions.

Reporter: "Today we're visiting with Keaton Jones and Doug Alverton in Benville, Kentucky, where local residents are preparing the town for a presidential debate. Keaton, what impact has the debate had on your life?"

Keaton: "Uh, well, I had lots of extra homework last spring because the teachers were so excited. And everybody in town seems to be working pretty hard to get ready."

The reporter swung toward me.

Reporter: "What about you, Doug? Any changes?"

Me: "Yeah. My favorite soccer field has been turned into a parking lot, and my mom's so busy that she's never home. I don't have much free time to play soccer or hang out at the pool."

Reporter: "Tough, huh?

Me: "Sure—there are days when I feel like roadkill." I heard people laughing. Having an audience was kind of cool. "Political roadkill," I added, with a big grin.

Reporter: "Does that mean neither of you has been inspired to consider a future in politics?"

Keaton shook his head. My mouth galloped on.

Me: "No way. Soccer's my game, not politics."

Reporter: "Why not both? Athletes sometimes go into politics. One of our own Kentucky senators was a professional football player."

Me (big smile, big laugh): "Maybe so, but soccer players are smarter than that."

That's when the interview ended, maybe because the reporter was laughing so hard. I guess Keaton and I were pretty good. The reporter gave each of us a T-shirt with WLXK-TV printed across the front.

My mother was impressed when she saw the shirt that evening. She was less enthusiastic after she saw my interview on the six o'clock news.

"Your mother's neglecting you and you feel like roadkill? Really, Doug." She huffed through the kitchen as we cleaned up the supper dishes.

I figured it might be good to get out of her way, so I wandered over to Keaton's house. He was always willing to go up against me with a soccer ball.

Right off the bat, I got two saves. Keaton gritted his teeth, and for his third kick, he tried a soft lob, the kind that forces me to jump. He got a little too much foot under it, and the ball went way over my head and landed in the driveway next door at old Mr. Finkey's house. Then it rolled into his rickety garage.

"No good," I crowed.

Keaton elbowed me as we started into the garage. "You won't be so lucky on the next one."

Mr. Finkey's house was sandwiched between Keaton's place and the Latture-Potensky household. Sophie's family was good friends with the old man. They drove him to the grocery store, and he let them put lots of junk in his garage.

It was a rickety old building, but Mr. Finkey had decorated the walls inside with a bunch of flags. Nothing red, white, and blue here. Sophie said they were flags from other countries. Mexico, China, Argentina. Places the old man had visited while he taught at Shelby College.

Under the flags, the floor was crammed with boxes.

When I tried to step over them, one box nicked the edge of my sneaker and flipped over. A bunch of old magazines slid out, and Keaton and I scrambled to pick them up.

If you asked me, those magazines looked pretty boring—no sports pictures on the cover—but Keaton got excited. He wiped the dust off one and started flipping pages.

"I could've used this for my extra credit project," Keaton said.

I took a second look. *"The International Socialist.* What kind of magazine is that?"

"Do you remember my project?"

"Yeah, yeah, yeah." Keaton was always doing something for extra credit. My mom wished I were more like him.

I thumbed through one of the magazines while Keaton told me more than I wanted to know.

"I did a report for Ms. Zadecki about the 1920 election. It all sounded pretty crazy. There was a political party I'd never heard of—the Socialists—and they had a candidate for president. Remember what I told you? The guy was in prison the whole time he was trying to get elected. A prisoner-for-president, and he got a million votes."

"Prisoner-for-president. That's weird. What'd he do—murder somebody?"

"Nah. He just said something he shouldn't have. Crazy, huh?"

"Yeah, crazy." I said impatiently. "Put that magazine back in the box and give me three more kicks. I'm gonna put you away for the night."

My big mouth. Keaton shoved three balls right past me, and I barely got my hands on the fourth.

Chapter 11

"If you can find something everyone agrees on, it's wrong."

- Morris "Mo" Udall

When I got home, my mother was parked at the kitchen table with a coffee cup. She was thumbing through a stack of news stories she'd printed off the Internet. I plopped beside her with a stack of peanut butter crackers and a cold glass of milk.

I glanced at the news stories. Most of them looked like long boring articles, but I spotted a picture of people marching and carrying signs.

"What's that about?" I asked. My mouth was a little too full, and I sprayed the picture with a layer of cracker crumbs.

My mother dusted off the crumbs and shot me a look. "That was a demonstration. It happened at a political event a few months ago."

"Are people going to show up in Benville during the debate to do that kind of thing?"

"Probably so. That's why I'm trying to think about what it might be like." She fanned out the pages so I could see more of them.

Right away I spotted a picture of people throwing rocks and bottles at policemen. "That's not a demonstration, is it? It looks crazy."

Mom nodded. "Sometimes political events are like soccer games—they take a wrong turn. Like when you and I watched the World Cup on TV and one player started throwing punches. He broke the rules."

It was my turn to be surprised. "You actually remember something from a soccer game?"

She laughed and poked me in the ribs. "I'm not a complete ditz when it comes to your number one priority in life. Can I assume that you're suddenly interested in some of my priorities?" She pointed to the news stories.

"Maybe," I answered. "Keaton and I were just talking about a guy a long time ago who ran for president while he was in jail. Keaton said the guy got arrested for something he said. Is that possible?"

My mom's a history buff. I could tell that I'd impressed her. I couldn't resist adding more. "1920. Presidential election."

"You," my mom said slowly. "You and Keaton have been talking about Eugene Debs and the 1920 election?"

I nodded as if I'd known the guy's name all along. "Sure. But I don't understand why he had to go to jail just for saying stuff."

Mom nodded. "People still argue about whether Mr. Debs should've been arrested. He gave speeches advising young men not to fight in World War I, and the government said he was guilty of sedition."

I made a face, and she explained. "Sedition means a person is trying to overthrow the government."

"Was he?"

Mom frowned. "Tough question. So tell me again, why were you and Keaton talking about this?"

I shrugged. "I tripped on a box in Finkey's garage and an old magazine fell out—about Socialists or something like that. Keaton wished he could've taken it to school for extra credit."

My mom's jaw dropped open. "There are Socialist magazines in Mr. Finkey's garage?"

I shrugged. "Might belong to Mr. Potensky. He keeps a bunch of junk in there."

"He's a *Socialist*?" She said it like it was a disease.

"Aw, I don't know," I said, scooting away from the table. "The magazines looked pretty old." I grabbed another glass of milk and headed for my room. My mother watched me go, admiring my knowledge of history.

It was turning into a weird kind of summer. At home, I looked like a genius at history. On the soccer field, I felt like a dimwit. Neither thing was my fault. Hanging out with Keaton made me look smart. Playing soccer with Tommy made me look stupid.

Mr. Kivacca still was interfering with the team. One practice, I'd be in the goal. Next time, it'd be Tommy.

We beat Lebanon and Berea, then lost to Jessamine and Somerset. Our record was 4-3, not even close to a perfect season. The way we were playing, we wouldn't have a prayer of beating Lexington.

My mother never listened to my gripes about the team, so I was glad when Keaton and I bumped into Mr. Potensky one day. The sun was blazing hot, and we'd just hopped off our bikes when he came out of his studio and closed the door. "Hey guys," he called across the yard. "How about a glass of lemonade?"

Mr. Potensky didn't have to ask twice. We headed for his porch and sank into wicker chairs while he went inside. He came back with a pitcher and three glasses.

"How's it going with summer soccer?" Mr. Potensky asked as he filled the glasses.

"Okay," Keaton shrugged. "Just not as good as we hoped."

"Aw, come on, Keaton," I interrupted. "We're wearing uniforms that look like prom dresses. And we've only won four games."

Mr. Potensky laughed.

I was on a roll. "The worst part is that we could've been terrific. If Tommy Kivacca's dad had kept his nose out of our business, Keaton could've scored about a hundred points by now. We'd be undefeated. We'd be ready to beat that Lexington team next Saturday."

I think Mr. Potensky wanted to hear more, but Keaton got embarrassed because I'd bragged on him. He changed the subject.

"How are you doing, Mr. Potensky?"

He shifted in his chair. "Strange kind of summer for me. Never had a deal like this, and I'm not sure I like the pressure. I've already been paid part of the commission price, and now I have to produce a sculpture that lives up to my sketches."

"Sculpture?" I asked. "I thought you did carvings."

Mr. Potensky laughed. "Now that there's money involved, it's sculpture. And it has a deadline. Not sure I can do it."

"Sure you can," Keaton said.

I nodded. And I kept my mouth shut about the fact that Mr. Potensky's own daughter had some doubts. Sophie had a way of being right about things ninety-nine percent of the time. It would be nice, I told myself, if—just for once—she could be wrong. If her dad really did have a deal that would make him rich and famous.

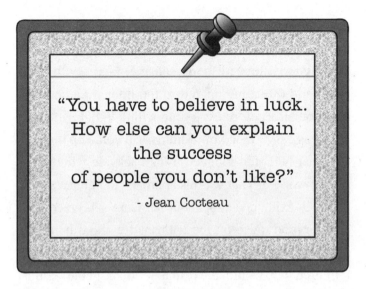

Chapter 12

"You have to believe in luck.
How else can you explain
the success
of people you don't like?"

- Jean Cocteau

There was one person in Benville who was already rich, and that was Tommy Kivacca's father. His printing plant was one of the town's biggest businesses. Keaton and I got to see it up close at the end of July. Our last week of working for the Berings, and what did we have to do? Deliver six huge boxes to Kivacca-land.

Mr. Bering drove the van, and when we got to the printing plant, Keaton and I hauled everything inside. On our way back out, I glanced into an office. Wow! There was a very fancy desk and thick carpet. Nobody at the desk, so I leaned in for a better view. That's when I saw something that made me clap a hand over my mouth to keep from laughing out loud.

I motioned for Keaton to follow, and we tiptoed inside. The office had a nice couch in one corner, and Tommy was flopped there, snoring. His mouth hung open, and one arm dangled to the floor. Keaton and I raced outside before exploding with laughter.

It was easy to see how Tommy had come up with the idea that he could lounge on his backside while other people worked. That was his approach to being a soccer goalie. It explained a lot about our team's 4-3 record.

Everybody else on the team had worked hard. We deserved a romp. An easy win with a big fat score. I figured we would have that kind of game against Abingdon, a town full of scrawny kids.

I figured wrong.

Half the Abingdon players had shot up six inches since our school game against them. The only guy who hadn't gotten taller had turned into a bundle of muscle. He was proud of himself and let us know it with a big, cocky laugh. When he saw our uniforms, he nearly busted a gut.

That wasn't the worst of it, though. With all the changes, Abingdon had turned into one of those teams that played soccer like it was a roller derby. Forget speed and nice footwork. Those guys were out to flatten us. They knew exactly how to do it without getting penalties. Any time Keaton got the ball, the cocky guy would tuck in his elbows and go for the ball. Wham! Keaton was on the ground, and the ball was gone.

Keaton thought soccer ought to be a finesse game, and he didn't go for the body blocks. Nixon, on the other hand, liked the idea of flattening people. Kind of hard for a guy who weighed less than a feather. He kept bouncing off the Abingdon guys.

And me? I was watching from the defensive end of the field, but not from the goal. Before the game, Mr. Kivacca had stood by Herb, muttering in his ear. When the line-up was called, Tommy was in the goal. I was a defender.

Every time Abingdon headed our way with the ball, I tried my best. I did fine until one of their shots bounced up after I stopped it. The ball grazed my thumb, and the ref called a handball.

My mistake. And Tommy would have to pay for it. Abingdon would get a penalty kick with nothing between them and the net except Tommy. He didn't like it one little bit. He muttered a lot of garbage in my direction. And when the guy gave a blasting kick, Tommy shuffled left. The ball went right. The score was Abingdon 1, Benville 0.

In the huddle at half time, I kept my eyes on the ground. Looked up just long enough to see Herb whip out the red notebook. He rattled off a list of everything we'd done wrong, until he got to me. "Doug," he said, "I know you're frustrated, but you're doing a good job of pressuring them on defense. Keep it up."

I raised my head a little. Enough to see Herb flip through the notebook one more time and take a nervous glance over his shoulder.

I looked in the same direction and caught sight of Mr. Kivacca. He had moved near the bleachers. And who was with him? My mother. She had finally come to one of my games, and what was she doing? Arguing with Tommy's father. Her hands were waving in the air like crazy.

Whatever was going on, my mother had managed to distract Mr. Kivacca from the game. Herb glanced in my direction. "Okay," he said suddenly. "I'm switching the line-up for the second half. Tommy's at defender, and Doug's in the goal." Tommy spluttered as I grabbed my gloves and ran onto the field.

The change helped a little. The Abingdon guys discovered that banging into Tommy was like hitting a brick wall. For once, he stood his ground.

Abingdon didn't score in the second half, and Keaton teamed up with Nixon to get the ball close to the net for us. But when the clock ran out, we still hadn't scored. Our record had dropped to 4-4, and the game with Lexington was less than two days away. We were on our way to a losing season.

I was dragging myself toward my mom's car when Tommy stopped me. "Alverton," he growled, "if you let anything get by you on Saturday, I'm beating you to a pulp."

"Oh, yeah, Kivacca? Well, if you ask me, you look like pulp."

I was thinking about throwing a few punches when Keaton cruised by and grabbed me by the arm. He pulled me toward my mom and started talking to her so cheerfully, you'd have thought our team won in a shutout. "Hey, Mrs. Alverton. Can Doug go with me to the college snack bar?"

Keaton never stopped thinking about food. "I'm dying for a chocolate shake," he told my mom.

It did sound good. Mom reached for her billfold. When she offered me a few bucks, I grabbed the money and headed for Keaton's car.

By the time his dad dropped us on campus, I realized I was starving. After I sucked down most of my shake, the day didn't seem half bad. It was about to get better.

Keaton and I nearly swallowed our straws when a man in a dark suit walked into the student center. "Looks like one of those Secret Service guys," Keaton whispered. "I heard that the agents have an office somewhere on campus."

The man headed up a set of stairs. In two seconds flat, we were following him.

By the time we crept up the stairs, the man was nowhere in sight. Down the hall, we saw a light go on in one office. A dark blue sign jutted from the wall above the doorway: SECURITY.

Pretty sly, I thought. The Secret Service didn't exactly go around advertising themselves.

The sign was enough to make Keaton lose his nerve. I marched past him. "For crying out loud, if you want a pin, let's get one."

The door to the office was open, and the man was working at a desk. He glanced up, and I said something stupid like, "Hi, how're you doing?"

The guy came around the desk. "Fine. What can I do for you?"

Suddenly words came tumbling out of Keaton. "I'm Keaton Jones, and this is Doug Alverton. We live near the campus, and, uh…."

Keaton caught a quick breath. "We'd be glad to help with anything you need." His voice trailed off. "You know, helping the town get ready for the debate."

You'd have thought it was the most normal thing in the world for two kids to barge into an office and act like they could be helpful to the U.S. Secret Service. The man smiled and stuck out his hand. "Steve Winston.

Glad to meet you, and I appreciate the offer." He shook hands with both of us.

It would've been extra cool if the guy had said something like, *Agent Steve Winston, U.S. Secret Service.* But maybe they only do that kind of thing in the movies.

Keaton couldn't screw up the courage to say anything else, so I decided it was my turn. "Do you know where we could get one of those pins—you know, with the stars on them?"

The guy eyed me, and I almost blurted out *No problem, no worry, sorry I asked.* But then he smiled and said, "I might have a couple of them." He turned to reach for a box on a shelf behind him.

While he fumbled with the lid, I took a quick look around the office. The place was nothing fancy. Just an old desk that had a phone, some ink pens, and a long yellow notepad.

I didn't mean to snoop, but in the split-second before the guy turned back around, I saw something written on the notepad.

Nicholas W. Potensky. Sophie's dad. His name was underlined in red.

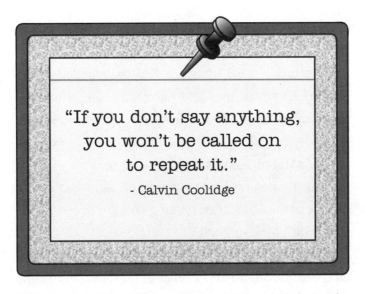

Chapter 13

"If you don't say anything, you won't be called on to repeat it."

- Calvin Coolidge

Keaton started burbling again as we headed down the stairs. "I can't believe it. We got a pin. That *agent* was terrific."

"Yeah," I muttered. "But he had a list. I saw...."

"Cool, huh?" Keaton held up his pin and studied it. "But it doesn't say anything about the Secret Service. You think it's the real thing?"

I checked my pin front and back. The thing had stars and stripes, a slogan about the U.S.A., and some funny little designs. Keaton was right. There was not one word about the Secret Service. And the man hadn't called himself an agent.

"Well," I said, "if they really are *secret*, they have to be careful about things."

"Yeah," Keaton agreed. "And this pin is exactly like the one Tommy has. He's going to be mad."

That brought me up short. Keaton intended to tell Tommy about the pins and our visit to the office. If I told Keaton about Mr. Potensky's name, he might blab that, too, and think it didn't matter. Maybe not, but what if Mr. Potensky had a secret?

With Keaton on a nonstop talking jag, I had plenty of time to think. I started making notes of my own, and they didn't look so good.

Number one: Mr. Potensky had kept his door closed at the studio all summer long. He acted like the commission was a big secret, but his own daughter had plenty of doubts.

Number two: he might be a Socialist, and my mother acted like that was one fat mark against him.

Number three: I'd seen Secret Service agents on Tenth Street, not far from Mr. Potensky's studio. Maybe they weren't looking for potholes.

Keaton babbled all the way home. The next day his motor mouth was still churning. He showed off the pin at soccer practice. Every guy oohed and aahed except Tommy, who pretended not to notice.

I worked extra hard in practice, hoping Herb would choose me to be the goalie against Lexington. He watched and scribbled in his notebook. At the end of practice, he said a dozen words: "Nice work. Go home and rest. We'll need your best effort tomorrow."

On Saturday morning, I shouldn't have been thinking about anything except how to beat those soccer hotshots from the city. It was the last game of the summer, and I needed to focus. But as I slid out of my mom's car at city park, my mind kept creeping toward Mr. Potensky and the Secret Service list.

It had rained during the night, but I barely noticed the pool of mud in the goalie box. I didn't catch the weird look in Tommy's eyes when he motioned the whole team toward one end of the field. He was holding a bright yellow bag from the New You beauty place, which seemed odd. My mom bought shampoo at New You.

Tommy herded us inside the restroom building and pulled a jar out of the bag, plus a box of latex gloves. "We're gonna wow 'em today," Tommy announced, sounding a lot like his father. "Our hair will be awesome. Half blue, half red."

He opened the jar, which was filled with some sort of blue cream. "This stuff's extreme," he said reverently. "Wear gloves and just get a dab on your fingers. Be careful putting it on your hair."

Most of the guys were awestruck. They reached for the gloves and started dibbling and dabbing with the blue goop. Nixon hung back, and Keaton shifted from one foot to the other, glancing in my direction.

"Use the blue stuff on half of your hair," Tommy announced. "Then dunk the other half in red Kool-Aid." He filled a plastic bowl with water and added two packs of Kool-Aid.

If the day or the week—or the entire summer—had turned out the way it was supposed to, I wouldn't have considered doing something stupid to my hair. But nothing had turned out right. It was going to take some kind of magic to win this game. Maybe a wild-hair surprise would be just enough to distract the Lexington guys. Get them a little off-balance.

I moved closer to the blue goop.

The other guys were careful. That wasn't my style.

I ignored the latex gloves and grabbed a handful of the blue stuff in my bare hands. Slathered it on one side of my head. I waited my turn to splash the other side of my head in the Kool-Aid bowl. Then a quick blot with paper towels, and I was out the door.

When Keaton and Nixon came out, each of them had just one thin streak of blue and one thin streak of red. At least I thought so. Keaton's hair was so dark that it was hard to see any kind of extra color.

I glanced around the field. Early in the summer, I'd dreamed about this day. Imagined that, for our last game, we would have a perfect sunny day. A perfect record and perfect uniforms. I imagined bleachers full of people ready to cheer us to victory over Lexington.

So much for dreaming. The real thing was a soggy field with a goalie box that looked like a mud pit. A team with a lousy 4-4 record. And the ugliest uniforms in the universe.

The bleachers were half empty. Keaton's parents sat on the edge of a tiny crowd of parents. My mom was beside them. Even she knew that this game was important. She was wearing a poncho because the bleachers were so wet.

Mr. Kivacca paced along the sidelines. As the first bunch of guys reached him, he started laughing like the hair thing was hilarious. But when Herb caught sight of us, he didn't exactly smile. He looked so mad that his moustache was quivering. I got the impression he was not a big fan of patriotic hair.

Keaton led the team through our usual warm-up routine. While I was practicing the zig-zag run, I saw Herb flipping through his red notebook.

Then, when we were supposed to be running in place, I picked a spot close to the sidelines. I saw Herb point to a page in his notebook and heard him speak to Mr. Kivacca. "Look at the numbers, sir. When Tommy has played sweeper, we've allowed only one score. He's brilliant at that position."

Brilliant? Herb was lobbying Mr. Kivacca. Trying to persuade him. "Tommy is the biggest man on the field, sir. Let's put that size to good use."

Mr. Kivacca sure liked the sound of that. Pretty soon, he was telling Tommy why he ought to be happy about taking a defensive position. I was crouched in the goal.

Two minutes into the game, Tommy got a penalty for tripping a Lexington player inside the box. Why couldn't he control his big feet? Lexington would get a penalty kick so close to the net that the guy could part my hair with the ball if he tried.

I swiped one glove across my forehead to make sure I wouldn't have any blue or red goop melting into my eyes. Planted my feet to get a good position in the mud.

At the exact second the guy kicked, I sprang and grabbed the ball while diving across the goal. I came down hard with mud splattering everywhere. But I hung onto the ball.

Our guys whooped and hollered. They came over to congratulate me, and I figured we were on top of things. But all that celebrating sent the Lexington guys into overdrive. Suddenly they were passing better, running faster, and kicking harder.

We stayed with them, but just before half, one of their guys got off a kick aimed at the top of the net. I leaped and felt the ball whiz past the tips of my fingers. The score was Lexington 1, Benville 0.

As I came down in a heap, I had one question. Would a taller guy have stopped it? Someone about the size of Tommy?

I might've spent the rest of the game in the dumps if it hadn't been for Nixon. Within the first minute of the second half, he got a great pass from Keaton and scored a goal.

That pulled our team back together, and we put up a real battle. I had five saves, and the Lexington goalie probably had six or seven. A great game, but our team needed to do more. The score still was tied.

With eight seconds on the clock, we got control of the ball. Herb got excited. "Push up," he hollered, waving his arms. "Everybody push up."

Our guys pressed toward the goal. Tommy glanced at me. Was he supposed to help defend our goal or head down the field to get in on the action? "Go on, Kivacca," I told him. "Go help them." He spun around and lumbered toward the others.

I was left standing alone in the mucky mess around our goal. If Lexington cleared the ball and came in my direction, I might be in big trouble.

When the clock showed three seconds, I saw something that spooked me. Lexington's best player was facing in my direction and moving toward the ball. Just as the guy tried to kick, my view was blocked by other players. I heard a loud thwack, followed by a blood-curdling scream.

The next thing I knew, the ref was raising his arms. Nixon and Keaton went crazy. Our team had scored. Then the clock ran out.

The scream, it turned out, had come from Tommy. Terrified of the Lexington guy's powerful kick, he had turned to run away. That's when the ball hit him in the backside and ricocheted into the net. He'd scored with a bun-ball. Who knows, maybe I'd have screamed, too, if that ball-rocket had smacked into me.

Tommy was a hero, and I was up to my ankles in mud. Still, our team had managed a victory and a winning season.

I ran down the field to join the mob of cheering Benville players. Tommy's face was bright red, and I couldn't tell whether he was celebrating or trying not to cry. The other guys tried to hoist him on their shoulders. They staggered two steps and collapsed in the mud.

They were rolling on the ground, laughing, when Herb joined us on the field. He shook hands with every single one of us, mud and all. When he stopped in front of me, Herb grinned and said, "Good job, Doug. You had some terrific saves."

My mother was smiling by the time I got to the sidelines. She whooped, "Way to go, Alverton," and held her arms open wide like she was ready to give me a hug.

I hesitated. Had she taken a good look at me? Mud covered my cleats, socks, and shinguards. The fancy uniform was plastered to my body. My patriotic hair was covered with brown gunk.

Mom cocked her head and gave me the once-over. I figured I was in for a lecture, but she wrapped her arms around me. "Nice work, Mr. Thrill in the 'Ville."

We slopped toward the car arm-in-arm. Mom opened the trunk and tossed in her mud-covered poncho. She handed me a giant plastic bag from the supply she kept in the trunk. I knew the routine and wrapped myself in plastic before sliding into the car.

At home, both of us left our shoes in the garage. Mom made me tiptoe straight to the shower. "Time to get rid of that glory mud—and the amazing stuff in your hair."

Things got a little less funny after that. In the shower, I noticed that my hands stayed blue no matter how much soap I rubbed on them. After the shower when I looked in the mirror, I got the shock of my life.

Here's the thing. The red Kool-Aid and blue goop were a lot more powerful than I'd expected. After all that scrubbing, half of me still had hair redder than a fire engine. The other half had sky blue hair sprouting from a navy scalp.

I had become a Thrill in the 'Ville alien.

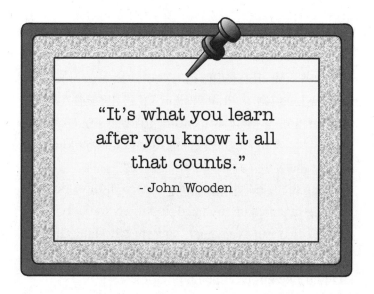

Chapter 14

"It's what you learn
after you know it all
that counts."

- John Wooden

Still planted in front of the mirror, I suddenly smiled. *All us players will have weird hair together*, I told myself.

Then I convinced Mom that my hair was a badge of honor for the victory over Lexington. I looked forward to the team meeting that night at the Pizza Palace.

By the time I got my first bite of pizza, I'd learned a few things. Our team had only three blond-headed players. The other two guys hadn't let the blue stuff touch their scalps. They'd splashed maybe three drops of red Kool-Aid on their hair. Nobody else looked as crazy as me.

The soccer team parents ate at a table in the corner of the Pizza Palace. Across the room, Mom kept giving me the eye. The minute we got home, she steered me to the bathroom. "What were you thinking, Doug? Did you follow the directions?"

I knew better than to answer those questions. I was quiet while she rubbed cold cream into my hair, then doused me with shampoo over the sink. Result number one: darker red, darker blue, oily hair.

Next she tried vinegar. Might as well have dumped flaming matches on my head, it burned so badly. Mom washed that out real quick and started slathering my head with mayonnaise. That cooled the flames, but I smelled like an overripe hamburger.

That's when my mom gave up. We rinsed my hair one more time and looked in the mirror. The red hair still was red. And the blue side? The hair was almost back to my normal blond, but the scalp underneath was still navy blue.

Mom studied me in the mirror and draped one arm across my shoulder. "You'll probably look normal by the time you're old enough to vote. Or win the World Cup in soccer." She laughed like a crazy woman as she walked out of the bathroom.

World Cup, right. My next big challenge was the school soccer team. The first practice was coming right up. I would have to face a whole bunch of guys with this alien head. I would be lining up for inspection by Coach Watkins.

Mr. Watkins is hard-core when it comes to soccer. He always holds the first practice at 7 a.m. on a Monday morning toward the end of summer break. He assigns push-ups to anyone whose attitude doesn't suit him. If he thought my hair showed attitude, I would spend time with my nose touching grass.

It's good to have friends on the team. Before I even got to practice, Nixon and Keaton had turned me into some kind of hero. They made sure that the guys who hadn't played summer league knew all about the Lexington game. My diving save on the penalty kick. The fact that we'd won.

Even Coach Watkins was respectful. He took one look at me and growled, "Heard you had a good summer, Alverton. I'll be expecting a lot from you this year."

Before I had time to decide whether that was good news or bad, the coach bellowed orders. "Okay, boys, let's get cracking. We've got ten days till school starts. Ten days to give your full attention to soccer. Ten days for you to whip those muscles into shape. Let's go, let's go."

Then we were running laps and dribbling around orange cones.

After practice was over, Keaton, Nixon, and I headed for our bikes. I was pooped, and Coach Watkins had ordered us to follow a super-nutritious diet, but Keaton and I had a tradition for the first day of practice—a doughnut-eating contest. It was time to initiate Nixon.

We rode down to the bakery, and can you believe it? The little guy beat us. Nixon scarfed five jelly doughnuts. Keaton and I quit at four.

With stomachs bulging, we roamed the streets of Benville on our bikes.

We pedaled down Main Street, where the bunting covered every store in sight. As we passed the ice cream shop, I saw somebody in the Uncle Sam costume. He was sitting on a brick wall out front, picking his nose. Sheesh.

At the soccer practice field near Shelby College, huge trucks had moved in. Each truck was connected to one of the zillion wires that sprouted from the utility pole at mid-field.

Keaton pointed toward the area that used to be a goalie box. "I hear they're saving that spot for the portable toilets." He and Nixon laughed.

Whether it was the doughnuts or the idea of toilets on top of the goalie box, I went to bed that night with a stomachache.

At midnight, I could hear my mother down the hall, still hammering the computer keys. Even after she gave up and went to bed, I kept tossing and turning. At two in the morning, I pulled on a pair of shorts and headed for the kitchen. A glass of milk seemed like a good idea.

Out the kitchen window and across the backyard, I saw a light burning in Mr. Potensky's studio. Why was he there so late?

My stomach wouldn't let me go to sleep. At three a.m., Mr. Potensky's lights were still glowing. Four a.m., then five. At six, when the sun started to come up, I gave up on sleeping. Six a.m. on a Saturday, and I was wide-awake. I wondered if Mr. Potensky felt as miserable as I did.

I glanced across the backyard again and saw somebody moving slowly through the wet grass. It was old Mr. Finkey, clutching his cane. He shuffled past his rickety garage and across his backyard toward Sophie's house. Then the old man turned and headed for Mr. Potensky's studio.

He knocked, the door opened, and Mr. Finkey disappeared inside. The door closed behind him.

What was going on?

I hurried outside, arms twitching with goose bumps.

There was no hedge near the studio for a hiding place, so I settled into the shrubbery next to Finkey's garage.

Twigs kept jabbing me in the ribs, so I slipped around to the front of the garage, looking for a better place to hide. That's when I saw a small yellow envelope stuck in the grass. I dashed to get it and raced back toward the garage.

No address on the front. I pulled out a card and found myself face-to-face with a drawing of a snake. Above it, there was one mysterious word.

Anaconda

And below the snake, an invitation to a meeting that night at the old man's house.

6 p.m., August 6, on Tenth Street
at the home of E. V. Finkey

I opened the card, hoping for an explanation. All I found was some kind of stupid quotation about wrestling.

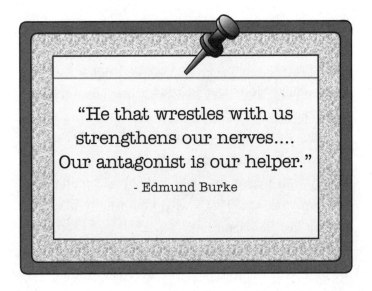

Chapter 15

"He that wrestles with us strengthens our nerves.... Our antagonist is our helper."

- Edmund Burke

The snake still was staring at me when I heard voices. Not too loud, but close enough to make me scrunch deeper into the shrubbery. Peeking through the hedge, I saw Mr. Finkey and Mr. Potensky climb into Mr. Potensky's old VW bus.

The grinding sound of the motor reminded me of their Saturday routine. The diner on Main Street offered a $3 breakfast every Saturday. Mr. Finkey liked to meet his friends there, and when he gave up driving, Mr. Potensky started taking him.

As the van moved out of sight, I skidded through the grass to the studio with that snake picture in my hand. The studio was locked.

I trudged home, hid the snake in my room, and flipped on cartoons. Still not sleepy, so I walked the floor, grabbing bites of dry cereal from a bowl on the counter. Mom was startled when she wandered downstairs in her bathrobe.

"What on earth are you doing out of bed this early?"

"Couldn't sleep," I grumbled. "I promised to spend the day with Keaton, but he'll probably sleep till noon."

Mom yawned. "That's what you usually like to do on your last free Saturday."

I shrugged. Suddenly the thought of spending the day with Keaton made me nervous. Should I try again to tell him about the list in the Secret Service office? Should I mention the locked studio and the snake thing?

As I watched my mother take her second cup of coffee back upstairs, I made a decision. I hustled out the front door and ran toward campus. I was almost out of breath by the time I raced into the student center and up the steps to the second floor.

There was a sign on the door of the Security office. CLOSED FOR THE WEEKEND. For Pete's sake, what if someone had a crisis on a Saturday?

I ran home. My mother was still in the shower, so I got on the phone and dialed a number. Keaton had said that the Secret Service had a permanent office somewhere up near Cincinnati. He'd found a number online and dared me to call it. I'd ignored the dare and kept the number.

I waited through four rings and then a mechanical voice came on, asking if I wanted to leave a message. The message didn't exactly say, *Hey, welcome to the Secret Service hotline*, but the mechanical voice sounded pretty official. Something about security. At the end, the voice said that if I was calling about an extreme emergency, I should contact my local 911 service.

Then the machine beeped. I could either hang up or start talking. My words tumbled out. "My name is...uh, uh. Well, the thing is, I'm calling from Benville, the town that's hosting the presidential debate. I don't know if this is.... Well, there's some kind of meeting in Benville tonight and, I don't know, but it might be—"

Click. The answering machine cut me short. Whew. I hadn't left my name or mentioned Tenth Street.

Then I remembered caller ID. The Secret Service could trace a call to the moon if they wanted to. They certainly could find one stupid kid in a town the size of Benville.

All morning, I hovered near the phone. Every time it rang, I pounced on the receiver before my mother could get it. Three sales calls. Nothing more.

By lunchtime, I figured the Secret Service wasn't going to call. When Keaton showed up with a basketball, I agreed to go over to his house to shoot a few rounds. After I missed thirteen consecutive shots and blamed it on the backboard, Keaton said I ought to go home and get back in bed. He was heading off to Lexington with his family for the evening.

So I did go home and immediately drifted into snooze-land. When I woke up with a start, the clock was flashing the time in my direction. 5:25 p.m.

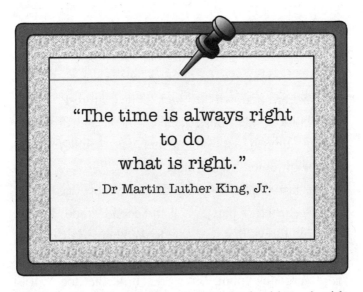

Chapter 16

"The time is always right
to do
what is right."
- Dr Martin Luther King, Jr.

5:30 I planted myself in the thick shrubbery beside Mr. Finkey's front yard.

5:41 I burrowed deeper into the hedge when I saw Mr. Finkey come out to sit on his front porch, wearing a bright red bowtie with his sweater.

5:46 Branches scratched my arms. Mr. Potensky pulled up at the curb in his old Volkswagen van and a bunch of men got out. One guy slid out of the front seat, his white hair flying in the breeze. Two others climbed out of the back seat. One had on a long-sleeved jacket that was the ugliest color of green I'd ever seen. Was it some kind of uniform? Mr. Potensky started across the yard, dressed all in black. I'd never seen him in anything but jeans.

5:53 Another car pulled up—a silvery gray thing that looked as long as a school bus. Four guys got out.

5:57 Two more cars, three more guys.

5:58 Farther down the block at the Latture-Potensky household, a side door squeaked open, and Professor Latture stepped out. Behind her was Sophie, with a weird expression on her face.

The last time I'd seen that expression was at her surprise birthday party back in second grade. Sophie had a meltdown that day. She locked herself in a closet and got a case of hiccups so bad that she had to go to the emergency room. Stress reaction, the doctor told her parents. It turned out that Sophie hated surprises, whether they were good or bad. When you're the smartest girl in the universe, a surprise is a slap in the face. Something you didn't guess ahead of time.

6:00 Mr. Potensky headed over to meet Sophie and her mother. About the time he reached them, another car pulled up at the curb on the opposite side of the street. Black compact car with out-of-state tags. The driver's door opened in my direction, and I saw the shoes first. Shiny black shoes. Then the guy eased out of the car. He was wearing a black suit despite the heat. White shirt, dark glasses, blue necktie.

His jacket fluttered once and, underneath, something glinted in the sunlight. My legs tightened.

6:01 The dark-glasses guy caught sight of Sophie and her parents. Mr. Potensky saw the man and stopped in his tracks. The guy spoke in a voice so low I could barely hear: "Nicholas Potensky, I've finally found you." The man's hand moved toward the edge of his jacket. I wanted to yell at the guy: *Wait a minute—this is America. You can't just shoot a guy without asking questions.*

6:02 Instead of yelling, I jumped. Leaped out of the shrubbery like the nerd-coach had taught me and went higher than I'd ever gone for a soccer ball. I tried to land on my feet between the guy and Mr. Potensky. Instead, I went sprawling, tripped by a small piece of rock that jutted from Mr. Finkey's yard. Kentucky limestone, I told myself as I nosed into the grass.

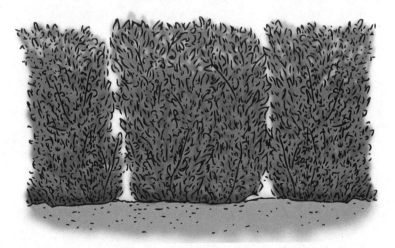

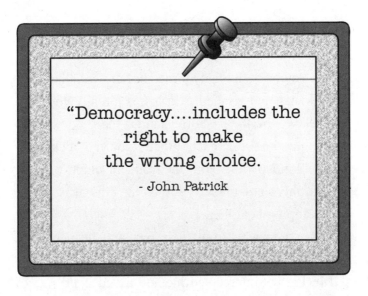

Chapter 17

"Democracy....includes the right to make the wrong choice.

- John Patrick

Without lifting my face, I knew the old men on Mr. Finkey's porch had stopped chattering to each other. I rolled to one side, just enough to get a good look under the man's jacket. His silver cell phone glinted in the late afternoon light.

I moaned and rolled my face back into the grass. Mr. Potensky knelt beside me and gently tugged me into a sitting position.

"You okay, Doug?" Mr. Potensky gave me a once-over.

"Fine," I muttered, pulling a piece of grass from my lip.

The other man bent close, studying me with an intensity that made me lean away from the two of them. I hoped he was staring at my red hair and blue scalp.

Mr. Potensky suddenly turned back toward the dark-glasses man and grinned. "Carlos, is it really you?"

The two of them shook hands, then stood right above me hugging each other. Not the awkward, wimpy kind of hug you get from an uncle or aunt who's only half-glad to see you. This was a big backslapping bear hug.

I scooted away from their feet and headed back toward the hole I had created in the hedge.

Mr. Finkey intercepted me and asked if I'd like to stay for dinner. I was trying to get away politely when he mentioned the fried chicken. "The caterer brought plenty, and I'd be glad to have you stay. I can set up an extra table for you and Nicholas's friend."

Fried chicken? My mom was heating leftovers.

Mr. Finkey gripped my elbow and steered me across the grass. "There's a bathroom just inside to the right. You wash up, and I'll call your mother to tell her you're having dinner here."

That's how I got a free meal of fried chicken, mashed potatoes, and coconut pie. How I got to know that Carlos Mendoza and Mr. Potensky had been best friends. How I learned that Mr. Potensky's grandfather had worked for the Socialist party in the 1920 election.

Mendoza sat with me at a little table off to the side, and he told me plenty. "Nicholas and I were inseparable when we started college," he said. I hoped it was okay for me to shovel down mashed potatoes while the guy talked. "But after he inherited all that Socialist memorabilia from his grandfather, Nicholas got obsessed with political history. That was all he ever wanted to talk about."

The agent made a face like he was in pain. "I was majoring in economics and thought socialism was the stupidest thing ever dreamed up. Nicholas and I argued all the time, and after we graduated, I didn't try to stay in touch with him. Then I got this assignment in Benville and found out he lived here. I decided to look him up. It's good to see him."

I wanted to ask *What assignment?* and *Who told you where Mr. Potensky lived?* But I figured that Mendoza was the type who liked to ask questions instead of answering them. I kept quiet.

After the coconut pie, old Mr. Finkey tapped a water glass to get everyone's attention. "I'm happy to call to order this meeting of Anaconda, the oldest literary and art fraternity in the state of Kentucky."

Art? I had called the Secret Service about a bunch of old men who had an art club?

Nobody seemed to notice how stupid I felt. They were hanging onto every word Mr. Finkey said. "I know how anxious you are to see the culmination of this project, so without further delay, let us proceed."

Mr. Finkey marched out the front door, and everyone followed. I figured I would slip through the hedge and go home, but when the group headed toward Mr. Potensky's studio, I decided to stick around.

Sophie's dad unlocked the door like it was no big deal. Everybody squeezed inside, and I elbowed my way toward the middle where Mr. Potensky usually carved. Something was there all right—something big—but it was covered with a thick gray cloth.

Mr. Finkey stood there with his fingers dancing around the cloth. He reached for a small sign.

The first three words, which seemed to be the most important, were in a foreign language. The words below them were in plain English. *A Balancing Act.* All the grown-ups oohed and aahed. I had no idea what was going on.

Mr. Finkey hoisted the sign higher. "This is the title Nicholas Potensky has chosen for his newest sculpture, which was commissioned by our Anaconda fraternity for the people of Benville in honor of the debate."

Uh-oh. It sounded like my mother was right. Mr. Potensky's commission was just another small-town project. He probably wasn't going to make a dime off the thing.

"I know you're anxious to see it," Mr. Finkey said. The other old men nodded and murmured. "But there is one more thing you need to know. The sketches Nicholas did for this project have won a competition at the Chavatel Gallery in Chicago. If he chooses to accept it," Mr. Finkey paused, "Nicholas will receive a very handsome stipend in addition to the modest commission that we provided. He also will have the opportunity to create a series of related sculptures for the Chavatel's permanent collection."

The way the old men whooped, I knew this must be a big deal. Somewhere to my left I heard a hiccup. Then Mr. Finkey yanked away the gray cloth.

Mendoza was scrunched against my right shoulder, and he let out a low whistle. "I had no idea Nicholas was that good," he said under his breath. "How did he do that?"

The gleaming white rock in front of us looked like some kind of magic act in progress. Like a giant pear balanced on its smallest end. Or a spinning top if you could freeze the motion. But a rock?

Okay, it might've been marble, but that's just a fancy, expensive kind of rock. And the way it was perched—well, I figured one little breath of air would send the whole thing crashing off the workbench.

Then I managed to get around to see the other side, and the rock looked totally different. From that angle, it looked as if an earthquake couldn't hurt it.

The shape tricked me, too. If I stared at the rock for a while, it didn't look like an upside-down-pear. More like a tree bending sideways in a storm. Or a fat, fancy question mark.

All the old men were circling the sculpture, just like me. Nobody paid much attention when Mr. Finkey started talking again about the title.

Who cares about the title, I told myself. *Just looking at the rock is enough.*

Somebody shoved a brochure in my hand. "This is the Artist's Statement," Mendoza told me. "You should read it."

I figured I wouldn't understand a single word, but who says no to the Secret Service?

When Mendoza headed off to congratulate Mr. Potensky, Sophie cornered me and held out a quarter. Her lips were pinched together and the hiccups trapped inside made her shoulders twitch every few seconds.

"You don't have to pay me this time," I told her. "I came because I wanted to."

She rolled her eyes and mumbled a few words between hiccups. "You…*hiccup*…don't understand…

hiccup...the title." She pointed to a row of itty-bitty letters along the edge of the quarter. I held it closer. *E Pluribus Unum*. The same three foreign words that were on the sign.

"That's our national motto," Sophie whispered through clenched teeth. A strangled hiccup followed, then more whispered words. "It means *Out of many, one*." She managed to get out the last part without a hiccup.

"Sure," I said, like I'd known it was the national motto. "But what does that have to do with the sculpture?"

Sophie answered with her lips still pressed together. "Many kinds of people...*hiccup*...one nation...*hiccup hiccup*...but it's delicate...*hiccup*... keeping things in balance."

Something clicked. Democracy is a balancing act. It's tough for our country to hold together all sorts of people. Grouchy folks like Mr. Bering. Workaholics like my mom. Rich bullies like Mr. Kivacca. Some days, it looks like the whole thing could topple. Then you look again and see the strength. The rock.

As the *Now-I-get-it* expression spread across my face, Sophie relaxed. Mistake. The hiccup that blew out of her mouth could have registered on the Richter scale. She bolted out of the studio.

Mr. Mendoza was saying his good-byes by then. When he headed for the door, he motioned me to follow. He stopped in the doorway, whipped out a business card, and pressed it into my hand. I looked at a fancy gold drawing and blue lettering. Carlos Mendoza, Federal Bureau of Investigation.

I should've said thank you. Instead I blurted out the first thing that popped into my head: "You're a G-man? I thought you were with the Secret Service."

For a second, Mr. Mendoza acted like he was mad. He narrowed his eyes and gave me a look. Then the guy laughed.

"Those agents aren't the only cool guys in town. Now listen up." Mr. Mendoza tapped the card in my hand.

"Hang on to that," he commanded. "Ten years from now, I want you to call me. By then, if you're still all la-di-da about the Secret Service, I'll give them your name. We're all looking for the same thing: gutsy types who have the courage to do the right thing."

With that, Mr. Mendoza shook my hand and left.

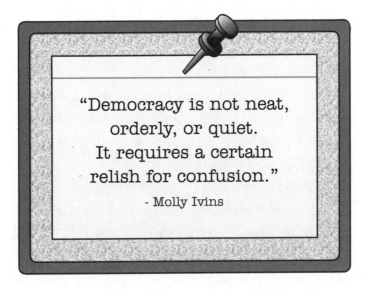

Chapter 18

"Democracy is not neat,
orderly, or quiet.
It requires a certain
relish for confusion."
- Molly Ivins

I guess I'll never know why Mr. Potensky's name was on that notepad, but one thing's for sure: his upside-down, fancy carving helped me understand the campaign trail when it finally arrived in town. It looked a lot like a circus path. Trucks and cars jammed the roads. Reporters with TV equipment blocked the sidewalks. So many people wore red, white, and blue that the town looked like a flag with feet.

Buses couldn't fight the traffic, so school was closed for the day.

Aunt Lana decided she just had to drive over from St. Louis to be in town on the day of the debate.

She called to say she was coming with a carload of Democrat friends. Mom said they could stay over and sleep in the basement rec room.

Mom left for work super-early that day, but I slept in. By the time I dragged myself out of bed, Aunt Lana and her friends had arrived. They were talking a mile a minute and drinking coffee.

I hugged my aunt and got out of there, heading to Keaton's house to meet him and Nixon. We planned to explore the debate circus together.

One part of the college campus was closed except to people who had security badges. Apparently, you had to put your name on a list and let the Secret Service whiz it through a bunch of computers to make sure you weren't some sort of criminal.

My mom's name had been cleared, and she had a security badge. Not me or Keaton or Nixon. Didn't matter, because there was plenty to see.

Not far from the student center, a group of college students marched around with duct tape on their mouths. They waved wads of play money and carried signs: DON'T LET BIG MONEY SILENCE MILLIONS OF SMALL VOICES: THINK, SPEAK, VOTE.

Beyond them, in front of a dorm, another bunch of students carried signs draped with bunting: SMALL GOVERNMENT + FREE ENTERPRISE = BIG OPPORTUNITIES.

The two groups of students didn't look too happy to see each other, so Keaton, Nixon, and I kept moving.

On a sidewalk near the hockey field, I saw two of the old guys from the Anaconda art club pushing a hospital bed. Another guy sat in the bed holding a poster: STOP THE RUNAWAY COST OF HEALTH CARE.

The Anaconda fellows seemed to be part of a wacky little parade. The three of us fell in step behind them. Which is how we ended up in Free Speech Park. It wasn't a park at all—just a big patch of grass with a stage and a microphone. A place where people could... well, speak. About any political issue at all.

When we got there, a woman stood at the microphone wearing a big blue button with silver lettering: MARS SOCIETY. She was telling people how important it was for Congress to keep giving money for space exploration. "Reaching for the stars," I heard the woman say, "is part of the American dream."

I couldn't believe it when I saw the next person in line for the microphone. It was Mr. Bering, the warthog man. I almost didn't recognize him. Up there on stage, he looked more scared than grumpy, and he was wearing an Army jacket. A man beside him had on the same kind of jacket and carried a sign. WE FOUGHT FOR YOU IN VIETNAM—DON'T CUT OUR BENEFITS NOW.

Oh, brother, I'd been rude to Mr. Bering a bunch of times. Nobody told me he was a war hero. What if he limped because somebody had shot him?

Keaton and Nixon were already racing toward a row of tables where people were giving out free stuff. I stayed near the stage long enough to hear Mr. Bering make a speech. It was super-short, and when he finished, I waved to get his attention. He glanced my way, and I gave a little salute.

He seemed to like that. At least I thought so. He saluted back and halfway smiled.

I had to run to catch up with Keaton and Nixon. They were standing at a table yakking with none other than Herb, our genius of a nerd-coach. He was handing out red, white, and blue Frisbees. A big sign behind him said: REGISTER TO VOTE.

At the next table, two college students sat in front of a fake tree. They were giving away bumper stickers. MAY THE FOREST BE WITH YOU—STOP CLEAR-CUT LOGGING.

I'd just collected a Frisbee and a bumper sticker when someone tapped me on the shoulder. It was Uncle Zeke, grinning. "I told your mom last month that I wasn't coming to Benville for the debate, but at the last minute I realized this was too good to miss. I brought our local GOP chairman."

The man beside him shook hands with me.

Uncle Zeke draped one arm across my shoulder. "Do you think your mom would mind if we went over to your house for a little while? Maybe grab a cup of coffee and make a sandwich."

"Mom's not home, and—" I began.

Uncle Zeke interrupted. "Oh, I know she's up to her eyeballs in work today, but I figured I could borrow your key and make myself at home."

I thought about Aunt Lana and all her Democrat friends crowded into our kitchen. They'd end up arguing with Uncle Zeke and his Republican buddy. Nothing wrong with that. It was like Benville would get two debates for the price of one.

"Sure," I told Uncle Zeke. "You won't need a key. Some other folks are there. They'll let you in."

As Uncle Zeke walked away, Keaton's eyebrows shot up. He knows my family. "I can't believe you did that," he said.

I shrugged. "They'll work it out."

As Keaton rolled his eyes, a familiar voice called my name. "Doug Alverton, you are just the person I need to see."

It was Ms. Zadecki. She was wearing a red and white striped shirt dotted with tiny blue stars. A blue folding chair was slung over her shoulder.

"Hi, Ms. Zadecki," I said. "Need some directions? Just keep walking toward the student center, and you'll find the area with the big TV screen."

My mom had explained plenty of stuff to me about the debate. People who didn't have a ticket to watch indoors could sit on the college lawn and see the whole thing on a huge TV screen. Until the debate started, there was free entertainment and a military band.

Ms. Zadecki was going to love it, but she didn't make a move. Just stood there staring at me. "That way," I told her, pointing for the second time.

"Thank you, Doug, but I need to discuss something else with you."

Uh-oh. What did she need to discuss? I was out of sixth grade, free and clear.

"I've nominated you to run for Student Council."

"You what?" I croaked. Student Council members were required to meet with the principal. Every month. In a small room. "Uh, thank you, ma'am, but I'm not sure I'm the right…."

Ms. Zadecki interrupted. "Certainly you are. The principal is expanding the council and asked me to suggest two of last year's sixth-graders. I told him that you and Sophie Latture-Potensky could represent a broad range of interests."

"Me and Sophie?" My words came out in a desperate whisper. Keaton and Nixon snickered.

Ms. Zadecki plowed forward. "I convinced the principal that it's high time the school put your energy to good use. Coach Watkins happened to be in the office, and he heartily agreed. In fact, he co-signed the nomination form. Your name is already on the ballot." She turned to walk away. "Have fun today, boys, and enjoy the debate."

Keaton and Nixon were howling with laughter as I heard a band start to play. I punched their arms and swung them around to face a flag that was flying above the campus near the TV screen. "Come on, guys," I said. "Show some respect. They're playing the national anthem."

★★★ THE END ★★★

A closer look at the WHO SAID IT? Wall:
The people behind the quotations

John F. Kennedy (1917-63) served as president of the United States. His famous statement that began "Ask not what your country can do for you," was part of his 1961 Inaugural address.

Bill Lyon (born 1936) is a sports columnist for *The Philadelphia Inquirer* newspaper and has written several books. He has been nominated six times for the prestigious Pulitzer Prize.

Raymond Moley (1886-1975) was a lawyer and college professor with a passion for politics. Early in the 1930s, he was an advisor and speechwriter for President Franklin Roosevelt. By the end of that decade, Mr. Moley had changed political parties and become a fierce critic of Mr. Roosevelt.

Leroy R. "Satchel" Paige (1906-82) is widely admired as one of the greatest baseball players of all time. In the 1940s, when segregation was common, he became the first black pitcher recruited to play in the American League. In the 1960s, he still was pitching scoreless innings, becoming the oldest person ever to play professional baseball.

Richard M. Nixon (1913-94) served as vice president for eight years (1953-61). After losing the 1962 election for governor of California, he vowed to leave politics forever and angrily told reporters, "You don't have Nixon to kick around any more, because, gentlemen, this is my last press conference." The comment became famous after Nixon returned to politics and was elected president in 1968. [Note: On Ms. Zadecki's wall, this quotation was amended to say "You *won't* have Nixon to kick around any more."]

Lawrence P. "Yogi" Berra (born 1925) is considered one of the greatest catchers ever to play professional baseball. He played for the New York Yankees and was named Most Valuable Player in the American League three times.

Eugène Ionesco (1909-94) became famous for writing plays that were funny in bizarre ways. His most popular play, *Rhinoceros*, tells the fictional story of a French town where all the residents are turning into rhinoceroses.

Al Smith (1873-1944) served three terms as governor of New York and was the 1928 Democratic candidate for president. He was proud of having come from a working-class family.

Mark Twain (1835-1910) is one of the most beloved authors ever born in the United States. One of his most famous novels is *Adventures of Huckleberry Finn.*

Harry Truman (1884-1972) was born on a farm in Missouri and had a habit of saying exactly what was on his mind without resorting to fancy phrases. He became a Senator in 1940 and was president from 1945 to 1953.

Morris "Mo" Udall (1922-98) represented Arizona in Congress for thirty years (1961-91). He took so much pleasure in telling jokes that a political columnist once said that Udall was "too funny to be President."

Jean Cocteau (1889-1963) was a native of France who wrote poems, novels, and movie scripts. He also was a painter and became friends with famous artists, including Pablo Picasso.

Calvin Coolidge (1872-1933) served as governor of Massachusetts and became president of the United States after the death of Warren Harding (1923). Mr. Coolidge was a man of few words and earned the nickname "Silent Cal." According to a popular story, a woman approached him one day and said, "Mr. President, I made a bet that I could get more than two words out of you." Coolidge replied, "You lose."

John Wooden (1910-2010) was an incredibly successful college basketball coach. His teams at the University of California in Los Angeles won ten NCAA national championships.

Edmund Burke (1729-97) was a native of Ireland who was elected to the British parliament. He favored rights for common people and sympathized with the American colonies when they sought independence.

Dr. Martin Luther King, Jr. (1929-68) was the principal leader of the Civil Rights movement in the United States in the 1950s and 1960s, pressing for black Americans to have equal rights.

John Patrick (1905-95) was abandoned by his parents as a youngster, and after a difficult life as a foster child and drifter, he became a noted playwright and screenwriter. His play *The Teahouse of the August Moon* was a hit on Broadway and won a Pulitzer Prize.

Molly Ivins (1944-2007) held journalism jobs in Texas and New York before launching a syndicated column that was published in 400 newspapers. She wrote about politics and American life with saucy humor.

Thrill in the 'Ville: **Questions for discussion**

Look at the following questions and have a discussion (or a debate!) with your friends.

1. Why would Doug's teacher, Ms. Zadecki, refer to the debate as a once-in-a-lifetime experience? Why, at the beginning of the story, does Doug disagree with her?

2. How did Doug's opinion of Herb Mumpower (tutor and soccer coach) change over the course of the story?

3. Have you ever seen political attack ads on television or the Internet? Do you think they are effective? Why or why not? If you were running for office, what kind of campaign ads would you have?

4. If you could meet one person in this story and ask a question, who would that person be? What would you ask?

5. In this book, political competition is compared to sports. Do you see any similarities between a soccer game and a political debate? What other things might sports and politics have in common?

6. Do you think Doug will try to get elected to a public office when he grows up? Why or why not? Would you vote for him?

7. In the story, Doug thinks Tommy Kivacca shows poor sportsmanship. How do you think Tommy might have been influenced by his father?

8. It sounds as if Doug's mother especially likes political leaders who care about funding for schools. If you were old enough vote, is there one issue or idea that would matter the most to you?

9. In the story, an artist creates a visual tribute to democracy. If you were asked to create a work of art that represents democracy, what would you draw or make?

10. How would you describe the personality of Mr. Potensky, the artist? If you had been with the Secret Service or F.B.I. in Benville, would you have been suspicious of him? Why or why not?

11. How does Doug change and grow over the course of this story?

12. Can you recommend a quote for the Who Said It wall?

The author is grateful to the Friends of the Boyle County (Ky.) Public Library for their strong commitment to literacy and civic education. In addition, the author wishes to thank several persons who provided feedback on the manuscript: Genetta Adair, Mary Jo Craft, Judy Dierker, Susan Donlon, Dawn Hardin, Diane Fisher Johnson, Anela Kinkade, Kate Leahey, Leigh Leslie, Rosanna Myers, Elisabeth Nesmith, Jerrie Oughton, Lois Quilligan, David Ray (U.S. Secret Service, Retired), Pam Ray, Elizabeth Thompson, Mary Trollinger, and Rhonda Washing. Any opinions expressed or implied by characters in this story are solely the responsibility of the author.

Patsi B. Trollinger knows about the hoopla that is part of a major political event. She hosted the media hall for the 2000 Vice Presidential debate held at Centre College in the small town of Danville, Kentucky. Now writing full time for young readers, Trollinger is happy to watch from the sidelines as another debate comes to Danville during the 2012 campaign season.

Trollinger is the author of *Perfect Timing*, which was honored as a Junior Library Guild selection. This picture book biography tells the story of Isaac Murphy, who rose from a childhood in slavery to become one of the nation's first sports superstars. www.patsibtrollinger.com

Elizabeth Thompson loves telling stories, whether they are expressed through the medium of writing or through visual art. A native of Danville, Kentucky and a graduate of Centre College, she experienced the 2000 Vice Presidential debate as a middle school student. www.elizabeththompsonstoryteller.com